Columbia 1942

ISBN: 9798393693169

1st Printing May 2023

3 6 9 12 15 18 21 24

Cover art and interior formatting by Calvin Cahail

Author picture by Robbie Mattson

Columbia 1942

By

James Hallaux

ALSO BY JAMES HALLAUX

WIND WITHOUT RAIN

(WITH CALVIN CAHAIL)

ASTORIA STEAK DELUXE!

ACKNOWLEDGEMENTS

Thanks to the wonderful people at Godfather's Book Store in Astoria and the Wednesday group.

Thanks to Phillip Holeman, Lenard Hansen, Larry & Dea Helligso, Blair Henningsgaard, Jim Mattila, Alan Robitsch, Bill Young, and Trygve Kelpp.

Thanks to Harry Antonio, copy editor extraordinaire.

Thanks to Calvin Cahail and all the staff at Sabertooth Books Services.

My love and thanks to Robbie and Oak.

This book is dedicated to

Mike Duncan

A true Astorian!

PROLOGUE

June 21, 1942

10:23 PM 8,000 yards offshore from Fort Stevens, near Astoria, Oregon.

The vessel emerges from the waters of the Pacific like a giant shark; massive, dark, deadly.

「潜望鏡を上げて」

"Periscope up."

「はい、大尉」

"Yes, Captain."

Peering into the scope, the Captain slowly walks the periscope in a 360′ circle.

潜望鏡を下げます。警報解除。表面化する準備をします。

"Periscope down. All clear. Prepare to surface."

はい、キャプテン

"Yes, Captain."

"Prepare to surface!" The klaxon rings out throughout the submarine. "Prepare to surface!" The effect is immediate. In 1 minute, all sailors at their stations, set, prepared.

A lethal naval war-machine is ready.

The war-machine, an I-class Japanese submarine, designation tag I-25. The I-25 is larger and longer than a US submarine but has smaller crew and officer quarters. It is a weapon; designed to do damage and death and all available space is used for these purposes.

The I-25, armed with Long Lance torpedoes, was the most destructive of the time and a 5.5-inch deck gun mounted on the stern. The gun has a range of 15,000 yards. Traveling from Yokosuka, Japan, to the Oregon coast, I-25 made the trip without refueling. With a range of 16,000 miles, it could make the same trip 3 more times, without refueling.

サーフェス、サーフェス

"Surface, surface." The klaxon again singing out loudly.

I-25 broke the surface.

オープンハッチ

"Open hatch."

ハッチが開きました、キャプテン。

"Hatch open, Captain."

砲手から甲板へ

"Gun crew to deck."

Before the deck is entirely above the waves, the gun crew at the deck gun, readying it for fire. Within 3 minutes, the distance and arc of shot determined and shell loaded.

デッキガン、ファイア!

"Deck gun, fire!"

The command to fire, given at 10:30 PM.

From the submarine, the exploding shells light up the shore for a kaleidoscope instant. Then darkness, next shell loaded, fired, then brilliant light. Darkness, light, darkness, light. The resonance from the exploding shells onshore echoes back to the submarine long after the flash. The sound seems to roll past Fort Stevens, then bounce off the higher dunes behind the Fort and come surging back. Past the Fort, low dunes, the beach, breakers and past the submarine, then lost in the dark, vastness of the Pacific. It isn't just a flash; it is more than that. It can be heard and felt.

The I-25 continued on the surface, following a northerly line of fire. 7 more shells fired. The attack lasted 20 minutes. It seemed like an eternity to the attackers and the attacked.

PART 1

CHAPTER 1

June 21, 1942 - 10:30 PM

Pvt. Bill Lowe had been sitting in the concrete watch shelter for 2 hours. He had another 4 hours to go before his shift ended. Even in June, the nights on Oregon beaches are cold and windy. Rather than keeping the cold out, the concrete shelter seems to bring the cold in and hold it. Bill thought it would be warmer if he stood outside.

Everyone in the Army referred to these shelters as 'pillboxes.' After a 6-hour shift, Bill felt exactly like a cold pill in a concrete box.

Bill swallows the last of the coffee in his Capital thermos. KAST radio in Astoria playing Glen Miller. Bill's small radio, a birthday gift from his parents, and strictly forbidden on watch, was necessary to keep from sleeping on watch, also forbidden. Bill's position; one of the forward watch posts at Fort Stevens. Sitting on a low dune above the beach, the site has an unobstructed 180' view of the

Pacific. With the Army-issued field glasses, heavy and hard to hold, Bill makes a sweep of the dark ocean. A couple of fishing boats off to the north, nothing to the south.

The flash came first. It blinds Bill, like his retinas exploded. The binoculars fall out of his hands, banging on his chest. Cutting into his skin, the thin cord around Bill's neck saves the binoculars from falling to the concrete floor.

'What the hell was that? Attack! Attack! Right now! Here!' Thousands of thoughts crash through Bill's mind.

The roar of the blast next. The concrete took most of it but Bill could feel the force of it on his face, through the observation opening and more frightening, in his chest. His mind went blank for several seconds; then his training brought him back.

"Command, command, we are under attack. Forward watch Post 7. Shells coming from the southwest. Repeat under attack. Confirm. Confirm."

"Post 7, we confirm. Saw it, heard it. Report, what do you see?"

"I can't see . . . my eyes . . . . ." But his sight is coming back. Afraid of another flash, Bill slowly raised the glasses to his eyes. It isn't what he saw; he hears it first, Japanese voices, command voices. Orders and response.

Then he sees it, the conning tower, the deck gun, and crew. And he hears the unmistakable sound of an artillery gun being loaded. Shell loaded into the breech; breech locked.

This time, Bill knew enough to lower the field glasses. Again, the flash, silence, force of blast, whistle of the shell overhead and finally, the detonation.

"Command, 2nd shell, fired from submarine deck gun 11,000 yards offshore. Sub looks like it is moving northward. Confirm."

"Confirmed. Are there other enemy vessels? Respond."

"None that I see, command."

All Bill can do is wait; there must be more shells coming. The wait; excruciating. Next, he hears the artillery gun being loaded; the submarine seems closer. Bill ducks under the pill box's open portion, hoping to block the flash and blast. Hunched down, he hears the whistle of the shell, coming close. Real close. Straight at his pillbox. Each second seems like an hour. And then it went overhead, inland, more to the North-East.

'This is it; they're landing. Right here, right in front of me. I don't care if I can't see other enemy vessels; they're out there. All I've got is a pistol and flashlight. That's it. They're landing, now.'

"Command, submarine directly offshore in front of me. Post 7. They're coming, now. Permission to withdraw." Bill's voice, high pitched and shrill.

"Post 7 repeat."

"Permission to withdraw."

"Post 7 repeat."

"Permission to withdraw."

"What?"

"They're coming now. I need to move back."

"Negative. You will stand your post."

"I'm not armed, other than a pistol. I don't have any defense. Need to fall back. Now."

"Private, this is Sargent McNary, stay there, or I will come down and run a bayonet through you. You will obey my order and stand your post. Do you understand my order?"

"Order understood."

Bill stood his post. Pistol cocked, waiting for an invasion that never came.

CHAPTER 2

June 21, 1942 – 10:35 PM

A brilliant burst of light in the night sky, the boom of an explosion, the duplicate echo of the detonation. Followed by a hollow silence, broken by the terrible whistle of an inbound shell. The new explosion, nearer, louder than the first.

The flashes of exploding shells and the sound of blasts can be seen and heard for miles. In Seaside, 16 miles south of the Fort, citizens line the Promenade above the beach watching and listening in small groups, unsure what is happening. The attack wakes people in Astoria and frightens others in nearby Warrenton, many searching for flashlights and weapons.

Fort Stevens is the first United States Fort fired upon by a foreign enemy since the War of 1812.

The Harbor Defense Command Post is located at Fort Stevens, in concrete bunkers dug deep into a high hill. Come an invasion, hell or high water, the Command Post can survive anything. It's a thing of beauty. The latest in instruments, everything the newest and best.

The defense gun batteries, however, are outdated, the Command Post, the exact opposite. The difference, widely known and commented on.

Harbor Defense Command Post, a vast room with several adjoining offices, is underground, buried in a high hill at the west end of 'battery row.' The Command Post is operational around the clock every day. Three 8-hour duty shifts. The Senior Duty officer at each shift has rank of Major or higher. Lieutenants or Captains are assigned the position of Junior Duty officer. Senior and Junior officers are supported by enlisted men. In the hushed, darkened room, these men stand over a huge, horizontal glass map of the entire lower Columbia River area. Lit from below, the map gives an eerie look to the darkened room. The men, wearing headphones and mouthpieces, hunch over the chart. Each man is a means of communication to different defense locations; ranging from Northwest Sector headquarters at Fort Lewis, Washington, to other coast observation stations from Canada to Mexico. And the 3 forts and gun batteries surrounding the mouth of the Columbia.

There is movement by the men from the glass map to the highly detailed regional maps hung around the room.

Teletype machines chatter in the background, muffled conversations between officers and enlisted men. These enlisted taking and returning communications from their various outposts. Sheltered, secret, hidden underground, the Command Post's work goes on 24 hours a day, 7 days a week.

But the Command Post isn't hushed and calm now. Not this night, June 21st; now it is bedlam.

Lieutenant Jay Kapp is getting ready for his duty shift; he will be the Junior Duty Officer at the Harbor Command Post. As is his custom, Lt. Kapp wanted to be early for duty. The first shell had him out the door of his quarters and into his jeep.

The command post is chaos. Kapp asked the obvious question to the first person he saw.

"Corporal, when do we return fire?"

"We don't, Lieutenant."

"What?"

"Lieutenant, the order from Harbor Defense Commander, Col. Daniel, is to keep searchlights off and not return fire."

"That Corporal, is damn unbelievable."

"Yes, it is Sir."

"Where is the Colonel?"

"At his quarters."

"I need a phone to Colonel Daniel."

"Yes, Lieutenant, use this. Good luck." The last part, sarcasm.

The Lieutenant calls the Colonel. The Colonel can't come to the phone.

"Goddammit! Who's the Senior Duty Officer?" Kapp, getting angrier by the minute.

"Major Dietrick."

"Where is he?"

"Don't know. Haven't seen him."

"Corporal, if I don't get a straight answer out of you soon, you'll spend the rest of the war in the stockade."

"I'm giving it straight, Sir, this is one hot mess. No one knows what's going on or who's in command. Near as I can figure, you're the highest-ranking officer here and that puts you in command . . . . . Sir."

Lt. Kapp goes on a rampage throughout the Command Post looking for Major Dietrick. Dietrick, nowhere to be found. Kapp tries again to get to Col. Daniel; Daniel unavailable. As the minutes tick by, Lt. Kapp realizes the Corporal is right; he is the ranking Duty Officer at the

Command Post. And with that, he alone is responsible for getting the Harbor Defense Commander's orders to Fort Canby and Fort Columbia on the Washington side of the River.

"Command orders: No searchlights, no return fire."

Lt. Kapp repeats those orders over and over and over.

The response; uniformly negative and uniformly obscene. In language that would make a Lutheran minister's ears fall off, battery commanders beg to return fire.

The responses are unusual; an order, after all, is an order. And this is the Commander's order and Lt. Kapp is the one to pass it on and demand that it be followed. Not an easy task.

The tension of the attack is one thing, and now the hostility from the Fort commanders and battery commanders is another thing. Lt. Kapp keeps restating the order to withhold fire again and again. A radar station from the Washington side of the River reports the incoming fire came from a range of 22,000 yards, 5,500 yards past the range of any onshore battery. In the next minute, several batteries report that the enemy vessel is 8,000 to 9,000 yards offshore, well within range of their guns. Contradictions, questions, and chaos ruled.

Major Faye Durheim, also from Harbor Defense, barged into the Command Post. Shouting, "Damn Sub, is in range. Fire, dammit fire!" Lt. Kapp repeated, for the 100th time, the Commander's orders.

"Dammit man, call the Commander in his quarters now; tell him they are in range. We must fire, now!"

"You are the senior officer, Major; you make the call," Lt. Kapp's reply.

The Major did make the call. And it is the first call answered by Harbor Defense Commander, Colonel Daniel.

"Colonel, the enemy is in range; I need your permission to fire. Give me the damn order."

"First off, Major, remember who you are talking to. My order stands: we will not return fire. The enemy is out of our range."

"Sir, that is incorrect. Batteries on both sides of the River report the enemy is within range. Give the order to fire and we will blow them out of the water. Give the order."

"Major Durheim, if we return fire, we will reveal our Battery's positions. We wi. . .."

"Hell, Commander, they are shelling Battery Russell right now. They know where the batteries are. This is a damn shooting war; we are under attack. Give the order to fight back. Give the order to fire."

The Commander hung up his phone, breaking contact with the Major. Major Durheim looked at the receiver in his hand for a long moment; then threw it against the wall. An enlisted man picked it up off the floor and returned it to the receiver.

During this time, the Command Center went silent. No one talked, no one answered the ringing phones. The silence continued for several more minutes and then it is broken. Tension, noise and fear, regain momentum.

CHAPTER 3

June 21, 1942 – 10:30 PM

Things are the same on the north shore of the Columbia River. At Fort Columbia, Battery Murphy gun crew is on alert, ready to return fire. Waiting for the order.

Lieutenant Allen is the on-duty Junior Officer for Battery Murphy. He is nearing the end of his watch. This Battery has a great view of the Oregon shoreline in front of Fort Stevens. Allen made a last sweep with his binoculars. What he saw, he couldn't un-seen. Just offshore, on the Oregon side, is the unmistakable shape of a submarine on the surface. Allen struggles to understand what his eyes are seeing. He can see the submarine crew on the deck. In the next instant, a brilliant flash lit up the Sub and the surrounding night. The attack begins.

Allen runs to the Fort's switchboard room and calls Harbor Command Post at Fort Stevens. He hears what everyone else heard.

"No return fire, no searchlights. Blackout conditions."

"No return fire, my ass! Sir."

"If there is any fire coming from any Washington batteries tonight, Lieutenant, it will be your ass and your court-marshal."

June 21, 1942 - 10:30 PM

Captain Ellesworth, the Commander of Battery Clark, at Fort Stevens, on the Oregon shore, has 'duty-quarters.' The quarters are in the Battery and they aren't much, just a table and cot, no chair. But it allowed him to get some shut eye during the long nights on duty. Tonight, Battery Clark is the 'ready battery.' Locked, loaded, ready to fire at a moment's notice.

Ellesworth checked on everyone and everything in his Battery. He is a 'stickler.' Other officers kid him and enlisted men talk behind his back. Ellesworth doesn't care. If needed for action, his team is ready.

Satisfied that all is in order, Ellesworth heads to his cot and a little light reading. He'd nabbed a Collier's magazine earlier in the day. Just as he is nodding off; magazine on his chest, reading glasses slipping off his nose, the first shell lands.

Ellesworth had gone to his cot fully dressed, even in his shoes. He shoots out of the cot and runs up the stairs to the battery plotting station 50 feet above his quarters. His team is already marking the source of the incoming shells. They have the position fixed and confirmed.

The Captain needs the order to fire. The call goes out to Harbor Defense Command.

"Lieutenant Kapp, this is Captain Ellesworth, Battery Clark. Target fixed; we are ready to fire. I need the Harbor Defense Command's order to fire."

"Captain Ellesworth, Colonel Daniel's orders are no searchlights and no return fire."

And like every other call Kapp got this night, the order is not believed, and then the order is repeated. The heated discussion moves next to who is the ranking officer on duty at Harbor Defense Command Post. It is Lt. Kapp and he is giving the order Colonel Daniel posted.

"Captain Ellesworth, for the 3rd time, I'm telling you the Commander's orders are no searchlights and no return fire. Do you understand the Commander's order?"

"Yes, I understand the totally bullshit order."

"What did you say, Captain?"

"Yes, I understand."

The tension in the command post; sky-high. Lt. Kapp is hoarse from yelling at the battery commanders. And his ears ring from battery commanders screaming at him. Colonel Daniel finally arrives at the Command Post from his quarters.

He made a difficult decision. It is a decision with only 2 outcomes, fire or withhold fire. At the beginning of the attack, he got conflicting reports; a radar station reported the submarine out of range for the gun batteries, but the gun battery commanders reported the submarine within range.

Colonel Daniel made the decision to withhold fire. He feels he made the right decision. He is the only person who thinks so.

Col. Daniel could hear Lt. Kapp arguing with a Battery Commander; this is the 4th time he's called. Daniel grabbed the phone away from Krom.

"Goddammit, listen to me. I have the Command; I made the decision and goddammit gave the order you are trying to disobey. No searchlights and withhold fire. If any fire comes from any battery, I will court-marshal the entire 249th Coast Artillery. Damn you."

And that is pretty much it.

The submarine gun crew made the deck gun water-tight, cleared the deck and the I-25 submarine submerged.

All the guns and all the men of the Harbor Defense
Command stood down and stood silent.

The next morning fog rolled into the coastlines of Oregon
and Washington. A mist started falling. The weather
matched the spirit of the men of Harbor Command on
both sides of the River.

All the training, all the waiting and nothing to show for it.
What a glorious night it could have been. All the Batteries
blasting away at a single target. The Sub hit for sure,
losing all hands, sunk to the bottom.

And the show of it. Dozens of brilliant flashes from both
sides of the Columbia, shells tracing across the night sky,
the impact of the shells. The horrendous sounds of the
guns. Windows broke from Seaside, Oregon to Long
Beach, Washington. Pictures falling off citizen's walls.

Stories that could be retold for a lifetime.

What is there to say now? Nothing. Like the guns, only
silence.

CHAPTER 4

June 21, 1942 – The Night of The Attack

The Twin Spruce Tavern, small, dark and a bit shabby, sits off the road under 2 towering Spruce trees. The owner, Tobie Tucker and his wife, Virginia, live across the road. The couple has been married 42 years and owned Twin Spruce for 35 years. They've been married so long, they've started to look like each other. Short, round with thinning hair. Tobie and Virginia treat the tavern like an extension of their living room. If you wanted to see the Tuckers, Mr. or Mrs., you never went to the house; you went to the tavern. They are always there. The tavern is where they worked, ate, drank, visited relatives, met with friends, got their mail. Lived their lives. If the Twin Spruce had space for a bedroom, they would have sold the house.

This Sunday night, like every Sunday Night, is 'Pot Roast Sandwich Night' at the Spruce. Pot roast, potatoes, and gravy over a soft white slice of bread, .75 cents. This 'Sandwich Night' got a late start in afternoon, due to the family Ford refusing to start after Tobie shopped for the roast at Piggly Wiggly.

"Tobie, what in the hell took you so long? I've been here by myself so long I'm about worn out."

"If we had a decent car instead of the piece o'crap your brother sold us, I wouldn't be late."

"Well, I'm not getting started on that roast until I sit here and have a drink," Virginia declared.

"That roast'll take a while."

"It will and now you mention it, Tobie; I'm not start'en until I have 2 drinks."

So, the late start. Then a quarrel at the pool table over who owed who, what. Tobie must step away from the bar to referee the squabble. Next, a heated discussion at the pinochle table regarding house rules. Again, Tobie leaves the bar. On his way back, he takes down the dartboard to avoid any fighting over that.

"Tobie, every damn time you're away from the bar, someone wants a damn beer. I need the roast and potatoes in the oven or this'll be a 'Raw Pot Roast' night at the Spruce." Virginia is getting miffed; not a good way to go with Virginia.

But the pot roast gets done, the sandwiches served and more beer drunk. A party of 6 returning home from Tillamook comes in late and eats up the rest of the taters and roast. The sandwiches are a little light by then, so they get a bowl of popcorn at no additional price.

'Stink' Smith sits at the bar by himself. The other patrons give 'Stink' a wide berth. He's nursed a single beer for 2 hours, a new record. 'Stink' is a regular at the Spruce;

actually, more like a lifer. He can't afford the .75 cents for the sandwich meal but had .25 cents for another beer. Virginia gave him a sandwich for free.

Virginia leaves around 9:30. Tobie says he'll be home in a bit. And that stretches into another hour. There are still 8 guys at the Twin Spruce, most of them at the bar, a couple at the pool table.

"What was that?"

"What was what?"

"That noise."

"Yeah, like a boom."

"More like a bang."

"What the hell is the difference between a boom and a bang?"

They all agreed on the next sound, a loud high-pitched whistle, that got louder and closer every second.

"I don't like the sound of___"

The shell landed 70 yards behind the Twin Spruce. Detonated on impact. The sound of the blast was ferocious, the shock wave blowing out the back door and all the windows in the tavern. And every window in a half-mile radius. The shell blew out a huge chunk of the back wall and roof. Anything on the wall is now on the floor.

After the blast, no one spoke. The ringing in their ears, too intense to do anything but stay still. Finally, Tobie says something.

"Is everybody OK?"

He calls out everyone's name and gets a muffled positive response from each. Later, most recalled they were amazed to be alive.

And then the spell is broken. Half the men head out the front door to their cars and homes. The other half move cautiously out of what used to be the back door. What used to be a dense Alder grove is now flat, the trees like giant pickup sticks scattered by a goliath. Using a flashlight, they find the shell crater and determine it is 6 feet deep and 20 feet in diameter.

All of this stops when the next shell came over. Farther away, more to the North-East. The men run, heading to their cars. Tobie to his house and Virginia.

That left 'Stink' at the bar, alone, sipping an Olympia beer he'd helped himself to.

'Hell, if I got to die, this as good a place as any.'

CHAPTER 5

June 21, 1942, The Night Of The Attack

The Japanese submarine I-31 surfaced and stood off the mouth of Willapa Bay 28 miles north of the Columbia River, awaiting a flash message from its sister submarine I-25.

The I-31 is identical to the I-25, except the I-31 interior has been reformatted for this specific operation. All but 2 torpedoes removed and replaced with 12 German-designed collapsible boats. Each boat can carry 2 men and a considerable amount of supplies. The sub crew had been thinned to the bare minimum to accommodate the 24 men who would crew the collapsible boats.

The plan is for the I-31 to maneuver as far as possible into Willapa Bay without running aground. The course had been plotted and checked for 6 months by a 2-man Japanese deep cover advance team. Because of the shallow level of the Bay, the I-31 needed to proceed on the surface. The I-31 would follow the route at a painfully slow speed, with depth soundings called out every 10 seconds.

The fail-safe point is the last place in the narrow channel that allows the submarine to turn around. The sub's mission is to off-load the 24 men, boats and supplies onto Willapa Bays waters, at night, without being detected.

Everything depends on time, tide, wind, and luck. A lot of luck.

The message came at 10:13 PM.

I-25 to I-31: our attack to begin in 17 minutes.

I-31 to I-25: message received.

June 22, 1942, early morning, the day after the attack.

The I-25 headed north, submerged, at moderate speed. The submarine surfaced once, briefly, to send a coded message to its companion sub, I-31.

The message came through exactly at the pre-determined time, to the second.

I-25 to I-31; our mission complete. Confirm and respond.

I-31 to I-25; Confirmed. Congratulations. Our mission continues. Confirm.

I-25; Confirmed and out.

Columbia River - 1942

The River, a huge theater with clouds rising from the horizon like a biblical backdrop. The forbidding clouds, a wall of darkness but at the very top, a patch of light blue light, mixed with the yellow of the sun that set an hour ago.

The River mirrors the sky, yellow gold on the top of the line of small waves. Dark blue just underneath the gold shine, beneath that deep, dark black.

Storm clouds, running fast, from the south, southwest. Separated from one another by brief patches of blue/gold. The bottom of the clouds dark blue, a shade away from black, heavy with rain. Seen from the Oregon side, looking north, the clouds dropping their rain load on Naselle.

In the midst of this grandeur, a freighter, 300 feet long, small in comparison, insignificant, heading upstream.

PART 2

CHAPTER 6

Trigby Theodore Newton bounded out of bed, full of life. *Early to bed, early to rise, makes a man . . . . . . well . . . . . Trigby* wasn't all that rich and, as his wife reminded him sometimes, not all that wise. But hell, smart enough to be a fully licensed, practicing physician. At just 4 years out of medical school, after working at the Salem hospital, Trig rented a storefront downtown to hang up his shingle and start his private practice. It'd take a couple of years but once he got the practice up and running, his earning years will start. *Who's ever heard of a poor doctor?*

That was before the Army grabbed him. The War changed everything.

The letter from the draft board came on a fine spring day. Trigby's wife, Janet, is planting bulbs alongside the small house they rent in Salem, Oregon. As their 3-year-old son, Jamie, tries to help. Trigby dozes in the hammock under the apple tree. Glasses on the top of his head, Life magazine across his chest. He's fallen asleep with a half-full glass of lemonade clutched in his hands on top of Life magazine. A bee lands on his cheek, rousing him with a start. He brushes the bee away; the motion causes the hammock to rock precariously. Awake but still drowsy, Trigby watched his wife, Janet and his son, Jamie.

"Janet, how much dirt has that kid ate?"

"Trigby, help me here, would you? You're lazing in that hammock like a Roman emperor. Do you want me to feed you some grapes? Jamie, put that down! Trigby, help me!"

The little boy held 1 of the smaller bulbs up to his mouth.

"Trigby, help me!"

"Yes, dear, I'm coming."

Trigby leans over the hammock's edge to put the lemonade on the ground. That's all it takes for the damn thing to twist 180 degrees, spilling him ass over tea kettle to the ground. His wife and son can't help but laugh.

The fall knocks Trigby's glasses off his head and somehow, they end up under his butt. He sits there, firmly planted on his ruined glasses, Life magazine soaked with lemonade, his family laughing uncontrollably. At him.

After a bit, the merriment quieted. Trigby puts on his glasses. One lens cracked; they sit cockeyed on his face.

The laughter starts up again. In time Trigby regains his footing and some of his composure.

All in all, wife and son think it is the funniest thing they'd ever seen.

Trigby Newton; tall, slender, with sandy red/blond hair that his wife badly cut as he sat in a kitchen chair. He bears a striking resemblance to his wife, Janet, also tall, slender, with sandy red/blond hair. Her hair is skillfully cut by her hairdresser.

At their wedding, one of Trigby's fraternity brothers noted, "Trigster, looks like you married your sister, man."

Trigby and Janet's son, Jamie, is small, round and what little hair he has is reddish blond. But only 3; no one doubted he would grow into a handsome replica of his parents.

The Newtons are a happy, handsome family. Everybody said so.

Trigby and his wife read the letter from the Draft Board, read it again. Janet started crying. They went through the 4 steps of Draft Notification; denial, fear, acceptance, and planning.

A week later, Trigby and Janet had their plans pretty much made. Trigby would join the Army in 3 weeks, induction to take place in Portland, Oregon. Basic training waived, Trigby is drafted into the Army because he is a doctor. Other men in the Army would fight, Trigby would repair the damage done to those soldiers.

From Portland, Trigby's first posting is Fort Stevens, located on the northern Oregon coast at the Columbia River's mouth. 120 miles from Salem. His rank is Lieutenant.

Sitting at their kitchen table, Janet and Trigby look and feel older. Not wiser, just older and scared. Ready to make the sacrifice, just like everybody else, but still scared.

"It just makes sense, Trig; I'll move back to my parent's house in Corvallis. I'll have my old room and their guest room becomes Jamie's."

"Didn't your room become your mom's sewing room?"

"Yes, and Dad started using the guest room as a home office. But they said they're excited to have Jamie and I live with them."

"Janet, of course, that's what they said. After a couple of months with this 3-year-old hell-raiser, they might move out!"

"That could very well happen," she said with a laugh. "But it does make the most sense."

"I just hate to see you give up all your efforts on this house and our garden."

"Our garden, Trig? Really, our garden? Lounging in the hammock, watching me work doesn't give you any ownership in the garden." Again, she says this with a chuckle and a smile.

CHAPTER 7

Trigby hates to admit it, but 3 months in, he kind of likes the Army. Or at least he's used to it. He enjoys the regiment of Army life, knowing what each day will bring. And the work is interesting. He went from a very small practice to being a part of a team responsible for the care of 2,500 people.

He enjoys most people he works with and they seem to like and respect Trigby. Fort Stevens has an unusual park-like setting. Very unusual for an Army base. Green and lush, with expansive parade grounds nestled among low sand dunes, the wide Columbia River on the Northern side and the mighty Pacific on the West. If not for the massive concrete bunkers and batteries, Fort Stevens could be mistaken for a resort. The thousands of men in uniform, the constant drilling and marching, also take away some of the vacation-time sense of the Fort. But local people from Astoria and Seaside come on the weekends for picnics alongside the parade grounds.

Trigby works an 8-hour shift unless something comes up; Jeep wrecks, mischarges at artillery practice, off-duty bar fights and other fisticuffs with locals or enlisted men. Or widespread outbreaks of flu, gonorrhea and syphilis.

He uses his off-duty time well. The Astoria Country Club kindly offered Officers the use of the golf course. Trigby had been a fair athlete in high school and college; medical school, residency, marriage and fatherhood took away any sports time. It is good to be back out on a golf course again. The fairways; a long expanse of brilliant green, with the ocean's roar on almost every hole. Trigby enjoys the local men he plays with and is a semi-regular with a group of Astoria doctors.

On Sundays, he tries to make it to Astoria for services at the Astorian First Christian Church. The familiar hymns, organ music and communion comfort him. The congregation members are welcoming and once they found out he is a doctor, Trigby became popular at the after-service coffee klatch. He listens kindly to complaints of lumbago, arthritis, allergies and dozens of other ailments, real or imagined.

One of the church elders, a long-time Astoria doctor, told Trigby, "thanks, kid, for giving me a breather. It's nice to have a cup of coffee after church, uninterrupted by doctoring. My suggestion to you; draw the line at removal of clothing to show you a rash, particularly if below the waist."

Trigby took the elder's advice.

All of this is bitter-sweet for Trigby. He misses his wife and son. They correspond almost every day, re-reading previous letters when the mail is delayed. Janet says she is fine but feels out of sorts, like she's go–ne back in time, living in her old room, following her parent's rules. Like a teenager again, not a mature mother with a child of her own. Janet's reoccurring complaint; her parents spoil Jamie.

There are phone calls; times pre-arranged so the precious calls aren't wasted. The telephone system within Fort Stevens is good, calls to the outside, iffy.

After 3 months, Trigby gets leave. And it is wonderful, together again, if only for 48 hours. Janet's parents kindly went to Portland for the weekend, they offered to take Jamie with them but Trigby declined. He reveled in having his family; wife and son, around him once more.

Another time Janet and Jamie drove down to see Trigby at the Fort. It was a bit of a trial for Janet. Her father wanted to drive them down, but Janet wanted just Jamie and herself to make the trip, using her father's new Ford. Janet couldn't tell if he was worried about her or his new Ford coupe.

"Daughter, it's a bad idea. Not safe for a woman to drive that new Wolf Creek Highway by herself with a 3-year-old in tow. Not safe."

Janet won the argument. She and Jamie, with enough baby supplies and clothing for 3 weeks, instead of 3 days, set off for the coast. Heading north from Corvallis on Hwy 99, Janet felt great. With her boy sitting on a pillow next to her on the wide bench front-seat; a feeling of independence and maturity swept over her. She is a full-grown woman setting out to see her husband, a brave man serving their country.

Hwy 99, straight as an arrow for the most part, goes through Monmouth, then Rickreal. Traffic heavy; agricultural trucks loaded with fruit and grain, freight trucks and much larger trucks loaded with logs. The log trucks frightened Janet. The timber, piled high and bulging over the sides, seems dangerous. How would you stop something with that heavy of a load? *"Hope they've got darn good brakes."*

At McMinnville, Janet pulled over at a roadside stand for a cup of apple juice for herself and Jamie. She knows the farming town well; her university years spent in McMinnville, at Linfield College. 5 miles later, Janet made a left turn onto State Hwy 47.

She continued her trek north on Hwy 47 through Carlton, Yamhill and Gaston. These towns, really villages, are the start of a revitalized wine industry in Oregon. An industry that had been almost wiped out during Prohibition. The road to recovery for Oregonian vintners would be a long one.

The next town of any size is Forest Grove, a pleasant small town. Janet thought about stopping for something to eat. '*If I keep stopping, we'll never get there!*' She continues driving, a woman on a mission.

After another hour, the Coast Range mountains are getting closer and Janet feels tired. She stops for a hamburger at Staley's Diner. Jamie doesn't wake up. The burger and coffee make Janet feel better, more alert. Which is good; the hard part of the trip is just ahead. She needs to get over the summit of the Coast Range mountains.

The uphill climb starts immediately after Staley's. The roadway makes graceful loops up the grade. Then through the new tunnel. Fully loaded log trucks roar toward her, moving Janet's car nearer and nearer to the side of the tunnel. Once through, back in daylight, Janet realizes she'd been holding her breath.

Now more loops, but these are going downhill, more relaxing than the uphill. But that doesn't last long. After a brief straight bit at Timber, the road curves upwards with a vengeance. A mean stretch of road; twisty, tight, some parts gravel, some parts washed out. Several stops for work crews. Janet used those times to loosen her grip on the steering wheel. '*Maybe Dad was right.*'

The worst is crossing the Nehalem River; the bridge just completed. It doesn't have all the safety rails installed, none on Janet's side. She held her breath again. After the village of Elsie, with the 40-foot Paul Bunyan wood statue, outside of Oney's restaurant, Janet starts to feel better. She is only 40 miles from Astoria and the road began to level out.

Passing Saddle Mountain, Janet knows she is home free. Hwy 26 merged with Hwy 101 and went through Seaside; Janet didn't stop. Following Trigby's directions, she made her way through Warrenton, then Hammond and through the gates of Fort Stevens.

Trigby met his family at the front gate. He'd been there, pacing, for an hour.

The Newton family together again. Trigby takes Jamie and Janet for a short tour of Fort Stevens and introduces them to fellow officers. They didn't stay long; Trig's wife and son are tired.

"Come on; I'll drive us downtown; you'll like where we're staying."

It's a relief for Janet not to drive. Not sure she will ever drive again; anywhere, ever.

Trigby did his family right, booked them a room at the Hotel Astoria. Soaring proudly over downtown Astoria the hotel is the highest building in the county and the entire Oregon Coast. 8 floors, 150 rooms and suites, dining room, bar and coffee shop; the hotel mixes Gothic Revival and Art Deco architecture.

Trigby met the manager of the Hotel Astoria at the Country Club. As it happened, the gentleman suffered from a bleeding ulcer, which Trigby found out within minutes of meeting him. Trig gave him a couple of diet tips and supplement suggestions. Apparently, they worked. When the man saw Trigby Newton on the reservation sheet, he upgraded them to a suite on the 7th floor.

"Trigby, this is marvelous. Can we afford it?"

"Only the best for my beautiful wife and handsome boy!" He told her later about the upgrade.

The next treat, room service. Jamie got a hamburger and fries; his parents, a bottle of champagne. Jamie wolfed down dinner like he hadn't been fed in a week and spent the next 45 minutes running around the 4-room suite. He loved hotel life.

Then a surprise for Janet. "Honey, we are going out for dinner."

"Where?"

"Here, downstairs. I think it's called the Frontier Room."

"Do they allow children? Are we taking Jamie?"

"Nope, just you and me. I've got a baby-sitter coming."

"Baby-sitter? Do you know this person? I'm not leaving Jamie with a stranger."

"Well, if I had my way, we'd lock him in the closet but I knew you'd object. The general manager's daughter will take care of Jamie. I think she'll meet your high standards."

And she did.

Janet changed and they went down to the hotel's dining room.

Dinner that night came as a welcome relief for Janet. It had been a long drive and a long time since she had been on a date.

"I could get used to this lifestyle, Trigby."

"Our son seems to have taken a liking to it."

"He has. Did you notice how he connected your call on the telephone to the burger and fries appearing?" Janet had to smile. "I caught him with the phone in his hand; I'm sure he was going for another burger."

The linen table service, candlelight, wine and good food, steaks, turned their table into its own small universe. Just the 2 of them; small talk, nothing serious, smiles, soft laughter.

It is a date. Not a first date, but a comfortable time between 2 good friends, lovers, husband and wife.

Dancing after dinner. Trigby, the dancer in the family. Janet, just along for the ride, and she enjoyed the ride. Her husband, a good enough dancer to make her look good. "Trig, I'm bushed," she said as the band ended their 3rd song, the dancers applauding the band. "Then off to our suite in the clouds, darling."

CHAPTER 8

Breakfast, the next morning, an in-suite, father and son affair. "Jamie, let's let Mom sleep in." Bacon and eggs for father; bacon and pancakes for the son. Pancakes with a lot of syrup. Trigby watches Jamie destroy his breakfast. Bacon went first, then the first pancake gone, in a tidal wave of syrup. Trigby cuts the first pancake into neat little squares; he didn't bother with the second. Jamie drenched it with syrup, used both hands, devoured it. He slows down on the third pancake.

Janet awoke to a son covered head to toe from what looked like a syrup shower. Bits of pancake clinging to most of him, his hair glue-like, sticking straight up. Jamie, trying to get into bed with her.

"No, no. Trigby, get him!"

Trigby got his son under control. In fact, he can't get his hands off the boy. They are stuck from the syrup.

"Trigby, what happened to Jamie?"

"Breakfast. I guess he could have used some adult supervision."

"Instead, he got you." Janet could tell it's time for her to get up.

After Jamie's bath, Janet's shower and Trigby's shave, the 3 stroll through downtown Astoria. Janet went into a couple of women's shops; the boys stayed outside on the sidewalk. Jamie's favorite thing to do in a store is to hide in the middle of circular clothes racks. Once, it took his mother 20 minutes to find him. For this offense, he is banned from stores.

Janet loves the clothes at Leon's but thought they were 'pricey.'

Commercial Street, the main shopping avenue of Astoria, is crowded with people and stores, bars and restaurants. Jamie says hi to everyone he passes. His parents received many congratulations on having such an outgoing child. Jamie and Trigby had the same thought, *outgoing indeed, just try to keep up with him!*

"Look at this sign in the window, Trig."

"A Woman's World is not Complete Until She Has A FUR! Saario Fur Shop."

Janet had her nose to the window, "what a beautiful coat."

"Unless we find 200 bucks on the sidewalk, your world will remain incomplete. Sorry."

Jamie did need new shoes. Gimre's Shoes had just what he needed and the opportunity to get a golden goose egg came with the purchase. Once the life-size goose replica's neck is pulled, the golden egg spills out the rear end of the goose.

Next, a maritime adventure for the Newtons. They walked on board the ferry that crossed the Columbia River from the 14th Street dock in Astoria to Megler on the north shore in Washington state.

Jamie loved it! Everything about it. Watching the cars drive on the ferry first, then the walk-ons. The smell of the River; creosote from the wooden pilings, diesel smell from the ferry engines, mixing with the automobile exhaust and blown away by the wind off the River. And the hustle and bustle of it all. One man directing cars into correct lanes; port side and then starboard. Another man chocks triangles of wood under the tires of vehicles.

The landing ramp went up and after the shrill blast of the boat's whistle, the ferry, Tourist 3, cast off. This craft is one of the newer ferries working the Astoria to Megler traffic. Built in 1931 in Astoria, the Tourist #3 holds 28 vehicles and 280 passengers. The car deck of the ferry has open areas, fore and aft. The next deck, up wide, steep stairs is the passenger deck. This deck covered most of the car deck below. The Coffee Shop is a big part of the passenger deck draw. Jamie has 2 doughnuts and a glass of chocolate milk.

"Janet, how much can this kid eat? He ate his bacon, my bacon and all the pancakes."

"Don't forget the gallon of syrup, dear."

"And the syrup, how much will he eat when he's 16?"

"More than he does now."

There is another treat for Jamie. He gets to meet the Captain of Tourist #3. Trigby was introduced to Captain Smith on the golf course. He suffered from lower back pain. Trigby prescribed an over-the-counter ointment and offered that Captain Smith should tee off from the forward tees and swing easier. The ointment and advice worked. Back pain went away and the Captain's handicap went down 2 strokes.

The ferry's wheelhouse is up a steep set of stairs from the passenger deck. A cable and sign block off all but AUTHORIZED PERSONNEL. Trigby removed the cable, led Jamie up the first step and replaced the cable. Janet could have joined the boys but another cup of coffee, alone, is what she wants.

The 'house' itself is small but well-trimmed, with gleaming woodwork and brass. The wheel; huge and appropriate to the size of the Captain. All 6 feet, 4 inches of Captain Smith, suited out in full maritime regalia, bent down to shake hands with the child and look him in the eye. "Welcome aboard, son."

To Jamie, the wheelhouse is the top of the world. The steep stairs up to the wheelhouse terrified him but he didn't show his fear. Now, this giant, dressed like a king, bends over to talk to him; almost too much for the little boy.

But then his father lifts him up so he can see out the windows. The view is tremendous, so high above the water, the River marine blue. The hotel they stayed at looked smaller now. Captain Smith and his father talked and Jamie listened. Not so much the words, just the sounds. Listening, watching the River, in his father's arms.

The Captain smoked a briar pipe. Trigby took his own pipe out of a jacket pocket. "Trigby, try my blend. They mix it for me at the Smoke Shop in Longview; damn long drive for tobacco but worth it. Now with gasoline allocations, I've had to cut back. Damn War."

Jamie knew his mother did not like his father smoking. Didn't like it, not at all. But he knew not to say anything. He is a big boy now, in a man's world.

"Like to take the wheel, young Newton?"

Jamie thought the Captain is speaking to his father. After a nudge from his dad, "Yes sir," comes out of Jamie's mouth. Trigby bought the newest Kodak camera for the trip and this moment is worth it. The picture of the tall, chiseled Captain holding his son in one hand and the boat's wheel in the other. Young Jamie's tiny hands on the pegs of the wheel. A huge smile and a look of amazement on his face. It is a picture that Trigby kept in his wallet for the rest of his life.

Jamie started the day wanting to be the man who operated the elevator at the hotel when he grew up; now he <u>knows</u> what he wants to be, a ferryboat Captain. Just like Captain Smith!

Trigby had planned on taking the family out for burgers at the Portway Tavern, considered by many to be the best burger in town. But Jamie fell asleep when they got back from the ferryboat and didn't wake up until much later. A cheese sandwich and tomato soup, room service again, all he needed. He fell asleep in the highchair. Trigby took him to bed.

CHAPTER 9

The next day, Sunday, dawned bright and clear. Janet got another morning of sleeping in late. Jamie and Trigby both had cereal for breakfast. Jamie's clean-up went much faster this day. They rode the elevator downstairs for a walk along the riverbank to blow some little boy steam off. They watched the ferry come in, unload, and go out. Jamie, content to stay on the pier watching all morning.

"Come on, Jamie, let's go and see if Mom's up." Jamie reluctantly agreed.

Trigby stops to get the Sunday Oregonian newspaper in the hotel gift shop for himself and a toy ferryboat for Jamie.

After his 2nd cup of coffee, Trig looked over the top of the newspaper to see his wife smiling at him.

"Hey, you're up! Good morning, honey, can I get you some coffee?"

"I'd love that. Where's Jamie?"

"Helping Mr. Anderson."

"Trigby, who's Mr. Anderson?"

"He's the guy that runs the elevator here."

"You left Jamie on the elevator?"

"Jamie wanted to and Anderson said it was OK. Nice guy."

Janet drank half her coffee, dressed hurriedly, and went out to retrieve her son.

Trigby didn't want to acknowledge it to himself, but he wanted to show off his beautiful wife and darling child at Church this morning. Jamie squirmed like a trapped hamster through the opening prayer and announcements. Finally, Trigby took the wiggle-worm downstairs to the Church nursery. The big room filled with toys and little kids. After the first few minutes, Jamie didn't notice his father had left.

After service, Trigby introduces Janet to all the parishioners he knows by name; those he didn't know introduced themselves. The congregation; warm and welcoming. The Pastor's wife escorted Janet and Trigby down the surprisingly steep stairs to the church dining hall in the basement.

The dining hall set up for the monthly after-service potluck lunch. 3 tables lined the rear of the hall, each 6 feet long, 18 feet of food! Not including desserts. Church mothers knew putting desserts out now would cause their children to dine in reverse order, dessert first!

Every item is homemade; to bring store-bought food to a church social is something only the Devil would try. First, appetizers; bread & butter pickles, sweet society cucumber chips and tomato relish, to mention just a few. After that, salads; Fisherman's salad, fruit salad, lettuce and fig salad with white figs and raisin sour cream dressing.

Mrs. Erickson brought her famous tomato aspic and shrimp gelatin salad and Mrs. Olsen, her molded crab meat salad. A huge pot of clam chowder has a whisper of steam swirling above it. Next to that; spareribs, smothered pork chops, fried chicken, 3 different salmon preparations, tuna noodle casserole and a liver loaf that no one seems to take credit for.

The array of breads and rolls, too many to list.

The Newton family, Minister Wes Layton and his wife, Rosemary, had the honor of going first. The 2 lines on both sides of the table make things move smoothly. Jamie, not tall enough to see all the temptations on the tables, could see enough. He is caught twice, grabbing food off the table and putting it directly into his mouth.

3 rows of tables for the diners filled the rest of the hall.

"This food is wonderful, Mrs. Layton," Janet said.

"Please call me Rosemary, dear; when you say Mrs. Layton, I think you are speaking to my Mother-in-law."

"Thank you, Rosemary. Please call me Janet. And I really mean it; this food is marvelous."

"Well, we try; food is second only to faith in a church. We do try hard and the results bear it out. I don't want to be prideful but we are a step up from the Methodists and Presbyterians, genuinely nice people but nary a good cook in either church. And the poor Baptists!"

"Food does seem to be important, Rosemary."

"Extremely important. And to be clear, we are no match for the Lutherans. Particularly Bethany Lutheran, on the east end of town. Goodness gracious, that group knows how to cook! If you have a chance to go there for a wedding, or even a funeral, by all means, go."

And from there, Janet learned a lot about Lutheran churches and neighborhoods in Astoria. The minister's wife had been raised Lutheran. Her father and grandfather are Lutheran ministers. Rosemary's parents didn't talk to their daughter for 2 years when she announced she was marrying a non-Lutheran. They did not attend the wedding.

"Rosemary, that must have been hard."

"It wasn't easy, Janet. We talk now but are not close."

Astoria has a dozen Lutheran churches due to the influx of Scandinavian immigrants at the turn of the century. Most of the male immigrants went into the fishing industry or some other maritime trade.

"Rosemary, that's a lot of Lutheran churches!"

"Astoria is a church town and a tavern town, in equal numbers. And don't get me started on brothels. Lutherans here are divided by their home country. Finns live and worship mostly in Union Town, by the docks. The Norwegians and Swedes are on the east end. And each neighborhood and Lutheran church is its own little clique. Although in Alderbrook, it's a mix of everything."

"Can a Finnish Lutheran go to a Norwegian Lutheran church?"

"Oh, certainly, Janet. They wouldn't bar entry to a Finn but a Finn wouldn't understand much of what is said at service."

"Services aren't in English?"

"Not all of them. Used to be none of them."

"Is this church based on nationality?"

"Gracious no, Janet. Here we welcome all kinds and a fine English heritage family like Mr. & Mrs. Trigby Newton suits us to a T."

Pastor Layton brought Janet's Lutheran learning to an end.

"Rosemary, enough of this Lutheran talk. They're putting out the desserts and coffee."

"Joseph, I might just become Lutheran again," Rosemary said with a smile and a wink toward Janet.

For dessert, Mrs. McIntyre, Mrs. Morrison and Mrs. Endicott laid out Jam Cake, Prune Cake and Dutch Apple Cake. This in addition to pies, cookies and candy.

Janet made a good impression by helping clear the tables. She offered to help with washing up but the Lunch Committee declined. They appreciated the offer but had their method and didn't need an outsider messing it up.

The Newton family spent the rest of the day driving around Astoria.

"Trigby, can we tour the town with gas rationing on?"

"Our last stop will be the Motor Pool at the Fort, Janet. I know a guy."

"Well, if you know a guy, Mr. Big Time, I guess we'll be OK. Can we drive up to the Column on the hill?"

"It would be great if we could. But we can't. The Astoria Column is closed due to the War. My parents took me there when I was a kid. Inside the Column is a spiral staircase with a million steps to the top. I went up to the top, twice."

"A million steps, twice; did you count the steps, Trigby?"

"Yes, I did, twice. Sorry we can't go up there, another cost of the damn War. On the other hand, I get out of carrying Jamie up those steps."

"Trig, what's it like on the top?"

"Windy, scary at first. The door to the walkway outside is hard to open because of the wind. When you get outside and the door slams behind you, that's the scary part. Some people, after climbing all those stairs, go right back down. They fight the door and then stand inside, getting themselves back together. And down they go."

"But that wasn't you, was it?"

"Well at first, I did have a little fright but my Dad was behind me. He got the door open and pushed me out. We crept around the cupola, with our backs to it, facing out."

"That doesn't square with the fearless hero I see before me."

"I was a kid, Janet. I do think my Dad was more scared than me. We both got our bearings after that first lap, we went around again, this time holding on to the railing. And that's where you get hooked."

"The view must be amazing."

"That's the word for it. Looking down, I could see Mom waving to us. Just a speck, I knew it was her, by the color of her scarf. You are up so high you can see forever. The ocean, the River, mountains to the east, high hills south, 30 miles away. Just incredible and almost unreal. Like a picture, but much, much better."

"Well, now I'm really sorry we can't go up there. Can we sneak up?"

"No, absolutely no sneaking, Janet."

"Chicken!"

Next, a tour of Astoria neighborhoods. Trigby hoped he could convince Janet that it would be best for everybody if she and Jamie moved to Astoria.

Alderbrook is the first neighborhood on the tour. A scenic, tightly knit community on the banks of the Columbia, Alderbrook sits at the far-east border of Astoria. A wide bay of the River had separated Alderbrook from Astoria proper. Now, with the bay filled in, railroad tracks and a roadway joined the neighborhood to Astoria.

"I like it, Trig. There's everything here. A school, grocery, park for Jamie, the River, everything I'd want. But it is a little remote."

"Remember, dear, we are just looking."

They toured the east end of Astoria on Harrison Avenue and the homes on Alameda in Union Town above the busy piers. And then the newer homes on the 'South Slope' of the hilly peninsula Astoria perches on.

The area and homes Janet liked best sat on the steep hill above downtown. Not the big houses near the top. But the more manageable one's midway up the hill. They found a small cottage for rent off 14th street on Grand. It is small and very cute.

"It looks like the upstairs bedroom has a river view."

"I think it does; I'll look into it, Janet, this week."

"You do that, Trig. I'm sure you know a guy."

The last stop is the Motor Pool. The tank filled; money changed hands. They took a different way out of Fort Stevens. Past an expansive green lawn, as long and wide as a football field. Majestic Victorian houses ring the meadow, the homes separated by tall trees. The grounds are used as parade grounds and a picnic area on special occasions; the 4th of July, Memorial Day (the Fort's cemetery just down the road) and the occasion of a new Fort commander.

"Wow, Trig, who lives here?"

"Senior officers."

"Aren't you an officer, Trig?

"Yes, dear, I'm an officer but 6 months in, I can't really be called a senior officer."

"Well, get senior fast. I'm ready to move!"

Trigby stopped again at the base hospital, mostly to show off his family.

The moment they walked through the door, a charge nurse called out.

"Lt. Newton, thank God you are here! We have surgeries in both #1 and #2, and now a private is in #3 with multiple stab wounds. Looks like he's been in a knife fight and lost."

"Well, my family is in town; I'm on leave, I don't think . ."

"Lieutenant, he won't bleed out on us but it will be a long wait. Better if he could be seen now."

Trigby notices all eyes in the room, including his wife and child's, are on him. He felt like the Lone Ranger coming to a small town, to save it.

"I'll scrub up, I'm sorry dear."

"No, they need you. We can wait."

Janet and Jamie didn't have to wait at the hospital. The Camp Commander, Colonel Daniel came in to have his ankle looked at. He'd twisted it getting out of a sand trap at the Country Club. After being told there isn't anyone available, he is introduced to Lt. Newton's wife and son. Informed that Lt. Newton offered to handle a dangerous wound case, despite being on leave, the Commander took Janet and Jamie to his grand quarters. They spent a pleasant afternoon with the Commander and his wife on the wide porch overlooking the parade grounds. The Commander taught Jamie how to march.

Meanwhile, Trigby, with a bit of swagger, came into #3 operating room. The wounded private, laying on his stomach on the gurney, looked up with a worried look on his face.

"OK, let me see what we have here," Trigby said.

It isn't really a dangerous case. There are wounds, 5 of them, made with what looks like a razor blade. All need stitches.

"You'll be all right, Private; tell me what happened. I'm interested."

"Well, Sir, my baby, she and I got in a bit of a tussle. I thought she loved me; she said so. But she got's a temper that can melt rocks. She went to the bathroom to cool off but comes after me with a razor. I'm lucky to get out alive."

"Nurse, are these wounds all we have?"

"Yes Doctor, we checked, all wounds are on the back, none on the front."

"Why is that Private? Just curious."

"'Cause I was running, Sir. I was scared."

Dinner that night, room service. Janet and Trig thought about the coffee shop but it was too much fun to watch Jamie take in the room service process. The whole thing mystified him; the phone call, ordering, the trolley arriving, then the complex set-up. The sides of the trolley lifted to make a table. Plates and utensils hidden underneath the trolley are placed on the table. And then, at last, the food. Jamie, fascinated by it all.

Janet and Jamie left the next day. She took Hwy 30; it runs along the Columbia, safe, fairly straight, in parts and more manageable than Wolf Creek. She made good time, arriving at her parents in time for dinner.

CHAPTER 10

After such a great time together, the renewed separation is hard on the Newton family. Especially for Jamie, he continually asks about his Daddy the first week back in Corvallis.

Janet and Trigby trade letters back and forth and there are weekly phone calls. But these things are merely salve over an open wound. It won't be good until they are together again.

"It doesn't sound right, us bitching about our small problems, in the middle of a World War."

She agreed with Trig, but his comment angered her. "Doesn't make it any better not to talk about it. And we only say it to ourselves."

Trigby thought he heard her crying on the other end of the line; the last thing he wanted to do. He jumped in with news of his latest housing hunt. Even that didn't come out positive. Housing is tight in Astoria for many reasons; built on a steep peninsula, there aren't many lots left suitable for additional homes. The Army, Navy and Coast Guard took up a lot of housing and the area is at full employment. Workers needed housing and had the money to pay for it. The best description for housing in Astoria, 'tough and expensive.'

And then, out of the blue, a break came.

Trigby had started playing golf with the Harbor Defense Commander, Colonel Daniel. He noticed that others weren't hasty to invite the Commander to join them for a round. Once Trigby asked Col. Daniel to join him to fill out a 4-some. After that, he didn't get invites coming his way either. The Colonel and Trigby usually played as a 2-some.

During most rounds, Trig answered medical questions from the Commander regarding himself, his family, relatives and friends. Trig asked his lawyer friend if he got demands for unpaid legal advice. "Yep, all the time. But not as often as you. Hey, I've got this rash . . . . . just kidding."

Trigby gave the Colonel a couple of tips (swing at 80%, hands ahead of the clubface at impact) that he'd received from the country club pro. He also didn't win any rounds. They are close, but the Colonel always comes out on top. Because Trigby lets him. He found it just as hard to hit a bad shot on purpose as it is to hit a good one. He didn't know which of these things or maybe something else got him the big break. It happened on the 4th hole. Score tied.

"Lt. Newton, there is an opening in Senior Officer Housing; I think it would be perfect for your wonderful wife and that darling boy of yours . . . . Johnny?"

"Jamie."

"Yes, Jamie, great lad."

'Jesus, I've jumped the line by a mile. Everybody is going to hate me.' This is the first thought that came to Trig's brain. He kept it to himself.

"I'd be honored, sir."

"Good. I believe it will be available on the first of the month. My adjutant will get in touch with you."

Brightness came back to the lives of Janet and Trigby. Plans made, movers hired, furniture bought, and decisions agreed on. All good things.

Janet's parents helped in many ways. They purchased the biggest help, a newish yellow Ford coupe, for their daughter and her family.

When they moved from Salem, Janet wanted to have the furnishings from their rental house stored in Corvallis.

Trigby wanted to store them in Salem. Trigby won that one.

Mayflower Moving picked up the items from storage in Salem, made another stop in Corvallis to pick up a smaller load from Janet and drove to Astoria (on Hwy 30), delivering the goods to City Storage in Astoria. Where they would be stored for a week until delivered to the Newton's new home at Fort Stevens.

Janet and Jamie wouldn't be coming to the new home until the next day due to a doctor's appointment for Janet. The delay grated on her.

"It's just a day, Janet. The boxes will be here, waiting for you."

"You'll be helping, Trig Newton!"

"Very busy at work, Janet, very busy."

Janet loved the new-to-her car. Her father had washed and waxed it. Checked the tires, including the spare. Checked the oil and window washing fluid. His daughter, *stubborn child*, decided to take the Wolf Creek Highway, again. Janet knew her route upset her parents. But she'd done it once and felt more comfortable now. And it is supposed to be faster.

Her parents will be down on the weekend to help, or at least keep Jamie under control. Janet loaded the car and her son, kissed Mom and Dad, and waved goodbye as she drove off.

At the Nehalem River bridge, a yellow Ford coupe and a loaded 18-wheel log truck collided head-on. The driver of the log truck received major but not critical injuries. The automobile's occupants, a woman and small child, died at the scene.

To this day, a mile West of the Nehalem River bridge, in the small Elsie cemetery, is a grave site, the headstone cracked and fallen. Inscribed on the headstone;

Janet Jane Newton

&

Jamie Samuel Newton

Bless them, Lord

CHAPTER 11

A big part of Trigby died when his wife and son died.

He went down a dark path, a path he didn't think he would return from. Trigby didn't take solace from anything or anybody. He infuriated Janet's parents and his own by not inviting them to the funeral at a gravesite in a remote cemetery. Trigby stood at the grave by himself. Alone, unknowing, shattered.

The only solace he received came from a bottle. His drinking was a problem when he and Janet started dating. It's the one condition Janet insisted on before accepting his proposal.

And Trigby stayed true to that pledge; he stopped drinking.

But he started again when drafted. It made the distance from Janet and Jamie a little easier. The loneliness, a little less.

After their deaths, the effect of his drinking became noticeable.

Alcohol became his crutch, then his savior, then his god.

Columbia River 1942

Cold, stormy, raining since early morning. Clouds, low almost to the water. The wind, hard from the northwest, 20 to 30 knots, roughing up the Columbia, sending waves crashing into the docks.

Everything in sight is grey. Sky, River, ships heading up and down the river, Tongue Point in the near distance; all grey. A thousand shades of grey.

From the Oregon side of the River, the Washington shore comes and goes as the fronts blow through. Now you see the other side, and then you don't.

In the early afternoon, there is a longer pause; how long, unsure. The River turns to glass. Colors come out; the buoy tender travels by with black and red hull, white wheelhouse and green trim. The Washington hills are dark green, almost black, with a frosting of white clouds on top. Still no sun.

Looking west, past Cape Disappointment, storm clouds on the horizon. More rough weather is coming. soon.

PART 3

CHAPTER 12

Latitude 46.620 8' North

Longitude 125.95 31' West

June 21, 1942, 11:45PM

The day after the attack on Fort Stevens.

The I-31 submarine surfaced after dark, off the Washington coast, 2 miles from Willapa Bay's wide entrance. The submarine, on the surface, creeps into the bay; once inside, the swells diminish, the water glassy, the night dark, no moon. 3 miles in, I-31 heading south at almost a walking speed. The reduced speed had to do with the narrow, twisting channel and the submarine's need to stay on course. Running aground or missing the tide would be disastrous to the mission. The sub also needed an area big enough to turn around.

The Japanese Captain and officers on the conning tower can see the distant lights of Bay Center, a small oyster and fishing village to the East. The Captain knows his location and how far he must go. Japan had been surveying the US West Coast for years. Their maps are every bit as good as US Naval maps. Without these charts and reconnaissance, this mission would not be possible. Even with these aids, the mission stands at extremely dangerous.

I-31 has no running lights and makes little noise. It is as dark and silent as the night.

「船首から南東に 300 ヤードの漁船。北へ」これはささやき声で言った。

"Fishing vessel, 300 yards southeast off the bow. Traveling north." This said in a whisper.

「船首から南東に 300 ヤードの漁船。北へ」これはささやき声で言った。

"Stop engine."

「エンジンを停止してください。」

"Full stop."

2 sailors raise their guns, aiming at the fishing boat.

The boat came within a hundred yards of the submarine. Fortunately for both parties, the I-31 remains unseen.

「ゆっくり先を行く」

"Ahead slow."

8 miles later, between the small towns of Oysterville and Nahcotta, Washington, the I-31 reached the fail-safe point. The fail-safe has 2 purposes; proceeding any further would be foolish, even deadly.

With the sub rocking gently, the unloading begins.

First, the 12 collapsible boats. They came in 2 parts, assembled on deck, in the dark. When constructed, the boats slipped into the water. 1 boat got away from handlers and had to be secured by a sailor who dove in after it.

Next, supplies; food, medicine, maps, compass, not much in the way of weapons, small arms, rifles and 2 ground-mounted machine guns. No explosives: they will be picked up later.

がんばって。

"Good luck."

Viel Glück auch Ihnen, Captain

"Good luck to you as well, Captain."

The boats, fully loaded, each manned by 2 men, 1 forward rowing, 1 aft, steering, heading south in the darkness for unoccupied Long Island and the start of their mission.

CHAPTER 13

The idea of a strike on America from inside its borders came from a German military attaché, Oberfuhrer Wolfgang Knorr, attached to the German embassy in Tokyo. He nursed the idea along and finally presented it to his superior, Obergruppenfuhrer Karl Nessler, based in Germany. The plan, detailed and well thought out; sent to Berlin in an encrypted radio burst.

Nessler turned it down out of hand. His reply, short and direct.

"German forces will not be used or directed by the Japanese military or government. Any attack on the United States in the Pacific or the West Coast of America will be implemented and prosecuted by Japanese, not German, forces."

And Obergruppenfuhrer Nessler wasn't finished. In a separate dispatch, he continued;

"Your orders, Oberfuhrer Knorr, are to engage with ranking members of Japan's armed services to learn new strategies and advances in weapons and training they may have achieved. If necessary, any combined German/Japanese military effort planning will be handled at a rank much higher than yours. Confirm your understanding of my orders and your mission."

Oberfuhrer Knorr learned his place and confirmed his understanding.

Another 6 months floated by when Obergruppenfuhrer Nessler was found to have, in addition to a lovely wife and 4 children, a Jewish mistress. His new posting, the Russian front.

With careful persistence, Knorr made his thoughts known to the German ambassador to Japan. The ambassador agreed with Knorr's plan and passed it on to contacts he had in Japan's military.

The attack would be a German/Japanese combined effort. German military had experience in lightning attacks with small forces over water and the boats needed for such a strike. Japan would supply transport to the Columbia River, a conduit to the interior of the American Northwest.

The raid would be a tribute to the Axis nation's collaboration.

The plan grew and changed with each new confidante Knorr and the German ambassador secured. Even with the changes, this plan made sense. To attack America on the West Coast beaches, a massive invasion force would be needed. Getting that force across the Pacific, problematic. It made more sense to attack inside the US borders with a small but potent force.

The idea wasn't to defeat America with an overwhelming invasion but a lightning strike showing Japan's strength and reach. Also, a huge blow to American home-front morale.

Several US sites were discussed. Puget Sound in Washington state. Not Seattle but deeper inland; Olympia, Washington, was a prime target for a time. Other inland ports; Aberdeen, Washington and Coos Bay, Oregon, came up for discussion. In California, Vallejo or Hayward, not San Francisco.

Several Canadian sites were also in the mix, but the attack needed to be on American soil for maximum effect. The Columbia River became the leading contender.

From earliest times, the Columbia was an essential source of food and commerce. Indian tribes along the River used fish as their primary source of sustenance; the River was also their means of transport and one of the gods of their religion.

With the coming of white men to the Columbia, life on the River changed. Not in a good way for the Indians. Disease and alcohol, in equal measure, took a terrible toll on the natives.

By the 1900's, the Chinook nation, the dominant tribe of the lower Columbia, was a ghost of its former glory.

In the 1940's, the Columbia River remained an important maritime highway for commerce and agriculture. Timber, logs and finished wood products from Northwest forests were sent worldwide from various Columbia River ports. Wheat from the Palouse region of eastern Washington, loaded on shallow-draft barges as far east as Lewiston, Idaho, traveled downriver to the tall granaries lining both sides of the Columbia. From there, the grain loaded onto ocean-going freighters with destinations worldwide.

Diminished from over-fishing at the turn of the century, the fishing industry remained an essential part of the economy along the River. Salmon, sturgeon, sardines, anchovies, crabs and clams all components of this vital industry. In addition to the fishing fleets, the industry included canneries (85 in 1940), boat builders, service suppliers for the boats and shippers that sent Columbia River fish products to domestic and worldwide markets. 20 miles north of the Columbia, Willapa Bay shipped ¼ of all oysters consumed in the western US states.

When the war started, the Columbia River became a crucial artery for the US war effort.

Henry Kaiser, one of America's premier industrialists, had a talent for getting things done. Big things, on time and on the money. His company was involved in building the Hoover, Bonneville and Grand Coulee dams in the 1930s and early '40s.

In 1938, Kaiser turned his attention to shipbuilding. England needed ships for the coming war with Germany. The island nation needed ships and Kaiser filled the need. From his shipyards in Portland, a new type of transport vessel came into being. Prefabricated on-site and then welded together in giant pieces. This assembly-line construction, based on Henry Ford's automobile business model.

The ships were known as Liberty ships. 441 feet long and 56 feet wide, they were efficient, durable, easy to build and inexpensive. With each completed ship, Kaiser and his team gained knowledge to build them faster. The record production scale was 10 days from laying the keel to launch. Kaiser's 76,000-person workforce, at 3 different facilities in Portland, became renowned for their efficiency.

In 1942 a new wartime need arose; aircraft carriers. And again, Kaiser had the solution. The new ship's naval classification was Casablanca Class Escort carriers; in common language, they were called 'Baby Escort Carriers.' The design is simple: install a wooden deck on top of a Liberty ship.

Each new carrier held 28 planes: Curtiss Helldivers, Grumman Avengers and Grumman Hellcats. The training for pilots and air crews was held at the US Naval Station, Tongue Point, in Astoria and at the Astoria municipal airport. Short-field take-offs and landings were practiced over and over. 441 feet is not a generous length for either take-off or landing.

After launching in Portland, Baby Carriers traveled the 127 river miles to Astoria on the coast and over the Columbia River bar to the Pacific. When sea trials were complete, planes landed for the first time on the deck of the carriers.

Landing a plane on 441 feet is difficult on dry land. On pitching and turning flight decks; it is a stomach-churning experience for the most accomplished pilot. Many crash landings on deck and in the water. Finally, with all planes accounted for, the Baby Carriers headed out for their battle missions.

4 miles wide at Astoria; the Columbia River narrows each mile inland. 40 miles inland, off the town of Skamokawa, the River channel narrows to only 100 yards wide. If a

ship, heading upstream or down, could be disabled or better, sunk in an appropriate chokepoint in the Columbia River, the effect would be devastating. Much needed finished vessels from the Kaiser shipyards would be stuck in Portland. Supplies shipped on the water destined for the shipyards in Portland would be stuck in Astoria. The disruption on fishing, grain, timber and many other parts of the economy, tremendous. In total, the distress to the Allied war effort, considerable.

And a huge blow to the US morale, particularly on the West Coast.

This was Oberfuhrer Knorr's plan in total. A swift, efficient attack on a major maritime conduit for America's war effort. With the added benefit of a shocking blow to American's sense of well-being.

This plan will need a person on the ground, deep cover, for months prior to the attack.

CHAPTER 14

Jukka Turpenen was the person selected as the deep cover agent for the beginning stages of an attack on Columbia River shipping. Jukka is not his name; he became Jukka through months of training and indoctrination. His given name is Gunther Emmerich; born in 1920 in Triberg, Germany. Gunther joined Nazi Youth when he turned 13; at 18, he enlisted in Nazi Officer Training through his college in Hamburg. At 21, he was recruited into the SS Corp.

Gunther has a gift for languages; in addition to German, he speaks Finnish, Dutch, English and French. Fluent in all, spoken and written.

This proficiency and Gunther's Aryan/Scandinavian features made him an ideal candidate for an immersion program running in the United States, in Oregon.

In 1941 Gunther, now Jukka, boarded a freighter out of Vaasa, Finland and weeks later arrived at the Quarantine Station across the Columbia River from Astoria, Oregon.

His Finnish passport helped him move through customs and his excellent health kept him out of quarantine.

The same day Jukka arrived at the QR Station, he walked west the 2 miles to the ferry landing in Megler, Washington and took the 40-minute ferry ride to Astoria. He stood on the deck, watching the River. It reminded him of a German autobahn, on water instead of pavement. Freighters, fishing vessels of all kinds, naval ships, ferries, all moving upstream and downstream, crossing the River from both sides. Noisy, busy, action everywhere one looked.

As the ferry neared Astoria, Jukka acknowledged the research he had read. Astoria is a working port, a working city. Granaries on the west end of the waterfront, canneries on piers everywhere. Onshore, as on the River, movement and labor.

Jukka knew his duty; to assimilate into this community.

PART 4

CHAPTER 15

Jukka's efforts in Astoria are his first deep-cover mission. To further his career in the SS, he must make it work. He knows his mission well, to quickly establish himself into the lower Columbia River region. And to find out as much as possible regarding the 3 forts surrounding the Columbia River's entrance. He is to acquire this positioning and knowledge for his superiors. This is the plan, or to be correct, this is as much as Jukka knows of the plan. His superiors will determine Jukka's need to know.

His 1st objective, to find lodging. Something close to the River, something cheap. He finds it at a boarding house, 3rd Street and Bond, 3 blocks from the River. A room and shared bath. Shared with everyone on his floor. 2 meals a day included: breakfast and dinner. It is the cheapest room and board he can find, but Jukka is still amazed at the expense.

Money isn't really a problem for Jukka; he has enough to last for 3 months, even without a job. If he can't support himself by then, he could ask his bosses for more money. But that would require a trip to Aberdeen, Washington, 86 miles north of Astoria, to make the request. And Jukka knew a dressing down would come from those same bosses, possibly a demotion and re-assignment back to Germany. To prevent any of this, he is frugal with money.

Jukka's language and accent aren't a problem either. The Astoria waterfront is a Babel of different tongues. Norwegian, Swedish, Danish, Finnish, Chinese, Japanese and, of course, English. Jukka is fluent in 5 languages. Fluent doesn't mean perfect. His Finnish accent isn't easily identified to a region.

When asked where he was born, Jukka always replies, "small village, far north." He could get by with speaking only Finnish, but the ability to speak English, a major plus.

For a man of Jukka's age and strength, Astoria's waterfront is a great place to find employment. Astoria has a wealth of natural resources; the River and Pacific Ocean, full of fish, the forested hills, full of uncut lumber. These natural resources need strong men to harvest them. Anyone who can fish with a net or fell a tree, can get a job.

The fishing industries, on the water and onshore, always need new hires. More accurately, new muscle with endurance and a high threshold for pain. The Columbia River enters the Pacific Ocean, 12 miles west of Astoria. It is one of the roughest bars in the world in terms of wrecked ships, approximately 2,000 and drowned seamen, over 6,000. These totals start from the mid-1700's. Record keeping in the early years, an iffy proposition. These totals could be way short.

Getting over the bar to the Pacific is one thing; getting back is another. And staying alive on the open ocean, between those 2 nightmares, is a hazardous task.

Fishing on the Columbia, by comparison, is easier and calmer. Not safe, just not as dangerous.

On a warm summer's day, gillnetting on the River seems almost pleasant. At 2AM in January, sleet coming down with a 40-knot gale, is a life-risking ordeal. Onshore, cannery work is also hard, with 12-to-16-hour days. An entry-level cannery job, for men, usually starts on the pallet crews. The hiring procedure is democratic. You are hired if your 2-man team can build a 6-foot stack of pallets faster than the current job holders.

Jukka hopes to find a suitable pallet partner; his other plan is to work on a fishing boat. He was looking for a pallet partner when he got lucky.

Veiko Tuustinen, owner and operator of the fishing vessel, Valhalla, had just lost his only mate to an accident with the chain-driven roller that brought the net in. It tore off the man's arm.

It wasn't much of a job interview. Veiko liked the look of the young man; strong and willing.

"Have you fished?"

"No, not commercially."

"I will teach you. Can you work, young man?"

"Yes, sir." Veiko being Swedish, and Jukka pretending to be Finnish; the conversation is in English.

"Do you work hard?"

"Yes, sir."

"Are you married?"

"No, sir."

"Good. Do you have family here?"

"No, sir." Most of the crews on fishing vessels are single. If there is an accident, and there are many, it makes the aftermath easier. And it makes the crews expendable.

"Good. You'll start tomorrow at 4PM to catch the tide."

"Yes, sir."

"And don't call me sir; call me Veiko."

"Yes, sir."

The next day, Jukka got to the dock at 3:30pm; he didn't want to be late on the first day of a new job. Veiko instructed Jukka on how he wanted the Valhalla set up prior to setting out. Everything in its place; neatness and cleanliness are the key points.

"A dirty boat can't catch fish, Jukka."

When the boat met Veiko's requirements, they cast off, with Jukka almost left on the dock. With the gap between the dock and boat growing swiftly, Jukka makes a heroic leap, landing on the gunwale and falling onto the deck.

"You are a leaper, Jukka! Let's see how you can fish. A nasty wind today, from the East; we will hide behind Tongue Point on 1st drift." Tongue Point is a peninsula that juts a half-mile into the Columbia at the East end of Astoria. It is an important base for both the Navy and Coast Guard. Veiko's plan; to use Tongue Point as a windbreak and let out a short-length net downriver from the Point, just outside the shipping channel. The River, calmer here, but it is a difficult dance to keep away from Navy and Coast Guard boats, plus the big ships traveling in the ship channel.

Like Veiko, Jukka has a plan too. He has a keen interest in Tongue Point and wants to get closer to the Navy and Coast Guard bases. He knew the Navy used Tongue Point as a base for reconnaissance seaplanes. The planes equipped with both sleds and wheels can get airborne from water and can land on water or runway. The Navy has huge hangars on land for the seaplanes, accessed by ramps that the planes rolled up from the River, their wheels activated.

The ship channel boundary is a line-of-sight guide from one buoy to another ¼ of a mile away. Red buoys on the right when going upriver, green buoys on the left going downriver. The channel is 300 yards wide and 43 feet deep. Veiko is confident he's outside the channel; he hopes everyone else agrees.

Like so many things in life, a good plan didn't work. The first drift netted no fish. "We will have to move to the other side of the ship channel, Jukka. Prepare for rough weather; we will be in the wind."

Jukka doesn't know how to prepare for rough weather. He recites a German prayer his mother taught him. As they moved north through the channel, protection of Tongue Point is lost. The wind howls out of the East at 20 knots, with gusts of 40. The Valhalla trembled at the onslaught of wind and waves. The River, angry, covered with white caps. The waves aren't the high waves of the ocean; these are smaller but relentless. Waves that break over the bow and wheelhouse are green in color. 'Green water' on the River is water that can sink boats and kill fishermen.

"Get ready, Jukka. We are heading back." Jukka wanted a life vest long before this but didn't want to look cowardly. Now, cowardly or not, he asks for a life vest.

"What do you want, Jukka? A vest, we're not going to drown. You think I kill you on your first day? Maybe next week, but today, nobody drowns."

As the Valhalla started its turn, a green water wave came over the bow and smashed the wheelhouse window. "What hell? What was that, Jukka?"

"A piece of wood, carried by the wave. It's here at my feet, like firewoo__, good God, look at yourself, sir."

"Don't have a mirror to see myself and I am operating the vessel to get us out of this damnable wind. Hard to see__

"Your forehead's bashed open, sir. Blood is in your eyes."

"Well, get me a towel. Take 2 big breaths; we will be out of this soon. If the boat doesn't sink and we don't drown."

Jukka got him a towel, took 2 deep breaths and said the prayer over and over.

The Valhalla pulled into the docks in Astoria.

"Jukka, tie us up, go into the locker and get the wood window."

While Jukka dug through the locker on the dock, Veiko opened the first aid kit hanging on the wall in the wheelhouse. He took out bandages, gauze, iodine; set them aside. Using a small metal mirror in the kit, he squinted at his image. *'Just a scratch. Big commotion, little scratch. Engine grease will do.'* Veiko opened the hatch to the engine compartment and removed a can of black, oily grease. He massaged the grease into his forehead and looked in the mirror. *'Good enough.'*

"Veiko, is this what you wanted?" Jukka held a wood panel in the shape of the wheelhouse window.

"Yes, it is; what else would it be? Put it in and nail it."

"I'll get the wood window in place and we can go to hospital."

"Hospital, Jukka? Hospital for such a small wound? No Jukka, we go fishing. We make money fishing, not sitting at the dock. Cast off now."

"Yes, Veiko, use the towel; blood is leaking out under all that grease."

"Where are we going, Veiko?" They headed west along the Astoria waterfront. Veiko is at the wheel behind the wooden window panel, leaning over to see out the glass window on his left.

"In front of Youngs Bay bridge, Jukka."

The Valhalla rounds Smith Point; the tip of the peninsula Astoria sat on. As soon as they are on the lee side of the point, the wind dropped, waves lessened. 3 drifts later, the fish locker, full.

"Let's head in, Jukka."

"Yes, sir!"

Veiko's wife made him go to the doctor. The wound took 14 stitches to close.

Jukka was truthful, he worked hard and Veiko appreciated it. The following 5 days went well.

"During the season, Jukka, any day that ends in a Y, is a fishing day."

"Yes, Veiko."

As it turns out, Jukka got very lucky with Veiko. A great boss and an excellent teacher of everything, on or under, the Columbia River. He is one of the few fishermen on the River to be an 'independent.' That means he can sell his catch to any of the 80 canneries on the lower Columbia. Most fishermen fish for 'their' cannery. Their cannery will loan money for boat repair or replacement, net repair or replacement, sustenance over the winter, etc. In return, the fisherman sells his catch only to that cannery, at a price the cannery sets. The system has some pluses and many minuses.

Jukka became Veiko's 1ˢᵗ and only mate and on-board cook.

"Make us bacon and eggs; there is some in the icebox."

This is Jukka's introduction to Valhalla's culinary traditions; only 4 items served. Coffee, and plenty of it, bacon, eggs and grilled cheese sandwiches. Jukka got the bacon going first; there was only room on the small propane stove for 1 pan.

'Does Veiko want his bacon crisp?' As he thought this, Jukka burned most of the bacon. He took more care with the eggs. Broke them carefully into a bowl. He tried to decide which way to prepare them for Veiko.

With Jukka below, hopefully making something edible; Veiko watches the gillnet. The net tight, the floats that held the net, bobbing underwater in places. This meant fish in the net, a lot of fish.

"Veiko, how do you want your eggs."

"On a plate, Jukka and soon!"

The gillnet hangs down from wooden floats made of red cedar, waxed to make them waterproof and buoyant. Light and flags sit on the top of the floats. The net hangs like a curtain from the floats, down 35 feet into the River,

1,500 feet in length. The nets were knitted from linen; some nets knitted by old-timer's hands, most machine-made.

Veiko and Jukka laid out the net at low water (low tide); it took them only 15 minutes. The net sat in the water for an hour and a half, closely watched by both men. Making sure it didn't get caught on rocks, dead-head logs or other boats. Retrieving the net takes 45 minutes.

26 feet long, with a breadth of 8 feet, the Valhalla is a 'bow picker.' The net came back on board over the bow. Powered by a Ford 6-cylinder engine, the Valhalla is a beautiful, sparkling wooden boat. Veiko had to admit, if only to himself, the Valhalla is the best boat on the River. He designed the craft himself; Matt Tolonen built it; Tolonen one of the dozen boat builders in the lower Columbia. Veiko had his first boat for 18 years and sold it for a good price after the Valhalla launched. The new boat would last 20 years, and make Veiko, if not a wealthy man, certainly a happy one.

It is heavy, hard work getting the net out of the water, fish picked out of the net and into the fish locker. Veiko works in the bow; his job made easier by a chain-driven 'skunk' roller, a metal pole laid horizontally across the bow, that rotated to help the net get on board. As the net came off the roller, Veiko plucked fish from the 8-inch mesh in which the fish's gills tangled. The fish, mostly salmon, are alive, wet and slimy, and hard to handle.

Veiko picked the fish out of the net and threw them into the fish locker.

After Veiko removes the fish, Jukka gets the first end of the net and pulls it back to the stern. Standing in the stern, he continued to pull the net back and fold it neatly into the locker. The net needed to go into the water untangled over the stern for the next drift. If it doesn't go into the water easily, it meant a stern talking to from Veiko.

There were usually 3 drifts, low water set, then flood tide and then high-water drift. The plan is to fish from low water through high water.

Jukka learned about the River, and learned about fishing and about Astoria, all from his mentor Veiko. They became a single unit on the boat, finishing each other sentences, seeming to know each other's thoughts.

In most ways, Jukka had a great life. Except for the lies. As their working relationship and personal friendship grew, Jukka answered the normal questions friends and employers ask with a lie. Sitting on the boat, drinking coffee, watching the floats on the net, Veiko asked,

"Jukka, tell me again where you come from."

On the spot, Jukka made up a village in far north Finland. That lie led to the next lie, which led to the next. Being untruthful to someone he respected, wore hard on Jukka. He had to report monthly to his contacts in Aberdeen, Washington. Jukka had to devise an excuse for a day-off from fishing every month. The 86-mile bus ride became easier with each trip, the deceit harder. The monthly excuses to miss a day of work, harder to come up with.

"Jukka, you need to pay attention to health. You are sick a lot. Eat more fish."

Jukka's primary mission is to blend into Astoria and the surrounding communities. He'd succeeded at that; the next directive; reconnaissance of the 3 forts around the mouth of the Columbia. Any time not spent on fishing is spent visiting a fort. Jukka was surprised at the lack of security. Some forts seemed to be used as parks by the locals, particularly Fort Stevens. On a weekend with nice weather, couples and families, Army and civilians roamed the grounds. Jukka blended in, usually taking a picnic lunch, camera and sketch books. He tried to look like a man on his day off. A man with a keen interest in gun batteries and troop deployment. Jukka also kept up on regional and national news, spending as much time as possible in the library, reading various newspapers.

The longer Jukka lived in Astoria, the more he liked the town and the people. He enjoyed the sense of freedom and the ability to achieve a better lifestyle for someone willing to work hard and take risks. He realized he didn't miss Germany, a hard thing for a German army officer to admit. Jukka had sworn allegiance to the Fuhrer and the German Army; he would not betray that trust.

But doubts started creeping into his mind.

CHAPTER 16

The monthly trip to Aberdeen, Washington, is always the same for Jukka. Up early to make the 6AM bus. He uses the time on the bus to make notes for his oral report. The required paper report, hidden inside the lining of the small suitcase he carries. It is written in sophisticated code. At these meetings, Jukka gives his verbal statement, a condensed version of the written one. He goes to lunch by himself while his superiors read the coded version. When Jukka returns, there is a general discussion about the reports and new orders given.

Seated in the rear of the bus, on the way to Aberdeen, Jukka makes several pages of notes, corrections, crosses out some parts, adds others. When he is satisfied, Jukka memorizes the report. Then tears up the notes.

At the bus stop in Raymond, Washington, Jukka gets off the bus and throws half of the torn notes in a trash can. At the next stop, the tiny village of Artic, Washington, he throws the rest away. His official duties done' Jukka's thoughts turn to Dea. It's as if he'd closed a file drawer marked Germany and opened another marked Dea.

For most people, the Germany part would be the hardest. Intrigue, deceit, the considerable risk of being found out, being caught as a spy. But for Jukka, the difficult component of his life is Dea and her family.

'I love the woman. Her family has taken me in; Veiko and Helmi are kind and caring. How do I repay them? I repay with lies. I lie about who I am, lie about what I'm doing, lie about everything. If my superiors find out about Dea, I will be re-assigned. Here one day, gone the next. Gone from Dea, gone from this life in America.

The bus rolls on, giving Jukka time to think about a conversation with Veiko regarding a partnership. With his experience and standing in the community, Veiko could get a loan from his lodge, the Scandinavian Benevolent Society. Jukka would captain the new boat, hire a crew, and repay his part of the loan. Veiko would remain Captain of the Valhalla and find a new 1st mate.

'This is a great opportunity, Jukka thought. *If the war ends this year, I could grab this chance. A life with Dea, a boat of my own. A chance to make real money. But will the war end this year, next year, or ever?'*

The bus pulled into Aberdeen just after 9AM. Jukka walks from the bus station to a decrepit 3 story office building in a difficult part of town. Jukka stopped to look the building over from across the street. There is a ground-level smoke shop that never closes and a café that never seems to open. Next to the café, a doorway. Jukka spent a long moment looking at the door. Then he saw it, a red mark on the door jamb. This meant it is safe to proceed.

Jukka opens the door with a key and heads up the steep stairway. The 2nd store landing has a door, with a pebbled glass insert. Looking through the distorted glass, a deserted row of offices. Then another steep set of stairs. *'Always stairs!'* The 3rd floor landing, another locked door and another key to open it. The hallway is a long row of offices, each with a pebbled glass door. The smell is dust, despair and business plans gone elsewhere. The 4th door on the left had ABERDEEN IMPORT/EXPORT in black letters on the glass. Jukka's knock is answered by a man who looks like he's been a poetry professor for the last 40 years.

"Good morning, Jukka. I hope your trip was uneventful."

"Yes, it was, Mr. Smythe." The persona that each person played would not be dropped.

"Tea, Jukka? I also have awful pastry."

"Yes, to both, Mr. Smythe."

The office has a row of file cabinets and 2 desks. If searched, the file drawers would reveal years of invoices, order copies, business letters, catalogs, and copies of Police Gazette. They would describe a failing business, stumbling along.

The desks, more of the same. But more personal items amid the flotsam and jetson. Birthday cards, hand cream, hairspray, dozens of pens and pencils, paper clips and every other small thing an office desk collects.

In contrast to the stage dressings, the actual business of the office is well-hidden and carefully curated. Only the most necessary papers are saved and hidden in secret compartments in the file drawers and desks. These items can be collected and destroyed in 3 minutes. There is a weekly drill.

"We will meet with Mr. Anderson in his office; another person will be attending. Are you ready, Jukka?"

'Another person, who would that be?' Jukka did not like the sound of that, not at all.

Anderson's office is a contrast to the 1st larger room. Still old and time-worn but small, organized, with a sense of efficiency. A man Jukka had not seen before, sat behind the desk. Anderson stood with a cup of coffee in his hand, appearing to be the sub-ordinate in this drama.

"Sit, Jukka," said the man behind the desk. There was only 1 chair, in front of the desk.

"Give Anderson your written report."

Jukka opened the suitcase, carefully removed the lining and gave the report to Anderson. Anderson paged through the report, then handed it to Smythe. Smythe took a bit longer reading and gave it to the newcomer.

"No, I don't need it." The newcomer is clearly senior to everyone else in the room. If you had to guess his age, it would be hard. Short hair, black mixed with grey, 2-day beard and a worn-out look and attitude. Except for his eyes; slate grey with a directness and energy that could cut through steel. If you had to guess his ethnicity, your 1st and only guess; German.

He spoke to Jukka directly, "I have come a long way, in rough conditions to discuss your mission." He said this in German. Every other meeting Jukka attended was in English.

"This mission is vital to the Fatherland and the Axis Powers. It will show the strength and reach of our combined forces. This mission depends on you, Unterstrumfuher. If you do your duty and the plan succeeds, your efforts will be noticed at the highest levels of government and SS. If you fail, you will most likely be shot by Americans; if not, certainly shot by German forces. Do you understand?

"Yes, Sir."

"The beginnings of this offensive have already begun. You were tasked with finding property on the Naselle River, on Parpilla Road. Property large enough to hide 24 men and 12 collapsible boats. Have you accomplished this goal?"

Jukka felt sweat rolling down his neck.

"Yes, yes . . . I have." Jukka had found the perfect property, available as a 6-month rental. The owner would be on a sabbatical in Florida. But Jukka had spoken with the owner 2 days ago; he told Jukka his sabbatical had been pushed back 4 months. Jukka neglected to share this news with anyone else.

"Excellent. Have you secured the 1,200 kilograms of explosives necessary for the mission? And the transport to. . . where is it . . . . yes, Grays River."

"Yes, I have a source for the explosives but they are not on the property. My only means of transport are the bus or my legs."

"Get him a used farm pick-up. Not good looking but runs good." The mysterious senior officer gave the order without looking at Smythe or Anderson.

Smythe was going to say something but thought better of it.

The man stared at Jukka with those slate-grey eyes. Nobody said anything for what seemed like an eternity.

Finally; "Untersturmfuhrer, you know your mission. Will you succeed?"

This time Jukka stood up and raised his arm. "Yes, sir. Heil Hitler."

"Save the politics for someone else. If you succeed, I will salute you; if you fail, I will shoot you."

PART 5

CHAPTER 17

Willapa Bay, off Long Island

After 4 hours of hard rowing, the 12 boats reached their destination; deserted Long Island. 5 miles long and 2 miles wide; the forested island sits at the south end of Willapa Bay.

The deploying of the collapsible boats and departure from the I-31 had been uneventful. The German leader of the raid, Obersturmbannfuhrer Friedrich Hann, had looked back once to the submarine's receding form, heading away, swallowed by the night.

He didn't watch with regret; he felt glad to be out of that stinking undersea coffin. The journey from Japan started tough due to the different cultures and languages. As the submarine crept across the North Pacific, it got worse. Hann's men weren't submariners; they were an elite SS assault team with 22 top-level missions to their credit.

Most of his men felt they had been buried alive under the waves.

The Germans hated the submarine, hated the food onboard (Japanese rations), and hated the Japanese sailors. The Axis Power's partisanship, shaky at best, even at the highest levels, did not exist with front-line troops.

It started with menacing looks, then a couple of close-quarter fistfights. A Japanese sailor showed up for watch with a broken arm. Wouldn't say how he got it. 2 days later, a German enlisted man went to the sick bay with a stab wound in his shoulder. He'd been asleep and didn't know who had stabbed him.

'Who in the hell had the idea of a combined force with no common language or military training?' Hann thought this from the begining; if he ever found out, he'd kill the bastard.

Halfway across the Pacific, things went completely out of control, with a fight involving a pipe wrench and a knife. The Japanese sailor died with the knife stuck in his neck and the German stormtrooper died of head wounds from the wrench. It appeared several different people had hit him.

Hann's second in command, Scharfuhrer Max Giese, disarmed all his men. Knives, razor blades, fingernail clippers, anything useful as a weapon. He also restricted them to a small area of the sub.

Both dead men buried at sea. Actually, undersea, they went out through an empty torpedo tube. Unfortunately, 1 of the men was the translator.

The daily meetings between Obersturmbannfuhrer Hann and Captain Koike of the I-31 had been tense from their first meeting. Oddly, the 2 murders had drawn both officers closer for the good of the mission. And the good of their careers.

Hann and Koike resolved that everyone under their command would conduct themselves with a strict military demeanor and efficiency. Any dereliction of this norm would be considered a court-martial offense.

That directive, announced over the sub's klaxon by each commander and repeated every morning, with both crew and troops at full attention. The violence stopped, but nothing else changed. Stormtroopers hated the sailors, and the sailors hated the troopers.

The only agreement on I-31, for German and Japanese officers and enlisted men – get this mission over as soon as possible.

Both deaths on board were reported as due to heart defects.

CHAPTER 18

Long Island is hard to see at night, revealed only by its flat, non-reflective surface. The water moves around the island, smooth in places, rippling with current and ruffled by the wind in others.

As the boats get closer, the island reveals more. Tall trees clustered together, darker than the night. The northern tip of Long Island, just a couple of feet above flood tide, is narrow and in the dead center of Willapa Bay. The island is wider to the south.

The boats follow the Stanley Channel, moving south, with Long Island to the west and the mainland to the east. The channel is tight, the tide changing from slack to low, the bay emptying fast. Paradise Point, their destination, sits at the island's widest point.

The first boat ran up on the beach, hauled onshore, supplies unloaded; the boat partially collapsed and carried a quarter of a mile inland. It takes 2 trips for each boat, boat first, then supplies and gear. Hann is in the first boat onshore; Giese, on the water, directs the remaining boats in, one by one. The crews waited their turn in the dark, ready to run at the first sign of trouble.

Giese thought this was taking longer than planned; Hahn thought it took an eternity. And then it is done. 23 men and supplies, 12 boats, beached, collapsed and moved inland, all completed in 45 minutes.

This is done in the dark, in complete silence, over rough ground. Dense forest, with blackberry bushes tearing at clothes. The boats and men, spread out and camouflaged. Cold rations, no fires, no lights, no talking. They will stay on the island for a day, hiding during the daylight, leaving at night.

CHAPTER 19

The next morning.

"That is a tremendous amount of mud, Oberstrum," said Scharfuher Giese.

"And a tiny amount of water," Oberstrumbannfuher Hann replied.

They are looking at Stanley Channel. Last night, Long Island had been surrounded by water, now surrounded by mud. Miles of it, as far as they can see north and south. A half-mile east, on the mainland, high forested hills come down to the water. Between the island and the hills, mud. A small trickle of water in the middle of the channel. Not enough to float a toy, much less a loaded, real boat.

"When is high tide tonight, Giese?"

"1AM, sir."

"Damn, I'd hoped we could leave earlier."

"We will need every inch of water to get us as far south as our plan requires, Oberstrum."

"Agreed."

The plan is to leave Long Island under cover of darkness, heading south in Stanley Channel, on the east side of a steep peninsula and the mainland. 5 miles in, the team should find the Naselle River and continue another 3 miles south to a small farm, prepared and waiting for their arrival.

That night, again in the dark, the boats carried to the beach, reassembled, supplies and gear brought to the beach, boats loaded and launched. Having done this exercise the night prior; the hope tonight is it will go faster. It takes much longer.

"If I could scream at them, they would move faster," Giese said to his Commander.

"What on earth is taking so damn long?"

"No screaming."

Finally, all boats loaded and, on the water, the procession begins. The boats, with muffled oars, move quickly, quietly, south through the night.

Finding the entrance to the Naselle River takes more time. The river changes daily, some minor changes, some major. After several false starts and groundings, the raiding party finds a narrow channel; deep enough to proceed. Just deep enough.

And the tide is changing from slack to low. The delays cost the party. They need to find their destination and find it quickly. The alternative is to drag the boats through the mud.

CHAPTER 20

"If we miss our landing, I will have your stripes, Giese."
Hann hissed this to his second-in-command. Their 2 boats
huddled together in the tight channel.

"This is a night I would give them to you, Oberstrum. But
we have not missed our site. It is just ahead."

"It was just ahead, 20 minutes ago."

"And now it is closer. Sir"

They were to look for a Finnish flag, tacked to a tree on
the south side of the river, 8 river-miles from their
encampment at Paradise Point.

Earlier, Giese had asked, "Why a Finnish flag?"

"A German flag deemed too obvious." There were times
Obersturmbannfuhrer Hann would like to slap Giese
across his face, using a pistol, not his hand. But that
would be foolish; Scharfuhrer Giese calm, confident and
the best leader of men Hann had ever known.

"The idea of the flag was dreamed up by the Japanese/German military masterminds in Tokyo. The property is to be secured by our advance agent." Hann said this in a less sarcastic tone. "If they had given us co-ordinates, we could be there by now, instead of playing find the flag, in the dark."

"We will find it. We must exercise patience, Obersturmbannfuhrer Hann."

The thought of slapping Giese arose again in Hann's mind, using a shovel rather than a pistol.

And then they find it; a Finnish flag hung from a branch leaning over the water. Hann's boat and another move to shore, the other boats hold back. Hann and 2 troopers walk slowly, carefully up the beach to a sloping lawn. Silence. No dogs, not a sound from the house. A single light burned inside.

Hann sends a trooper to each end of the cottage. He waits a moment and climbs the 2 stairs to a wooden deck that runs the length of the cottage. He inches past a wide summer glider and a couple of wooden Adirondack chairs. On the deck, Hann stands hidden in the darkness. He looks through a large picture window at a man sitting alone, in the middle of a dinner table. An overhead light shines down on him. The man sits looking at something on the table, perhaps reading a newspaper. Hann waits for the man to move. He doesn't; he can't.

The man, shot in the middle of his forehead.

It takes Hann a moment to realize what he saw. There is little blood, just a bright red hole in the man's head. The door at the end of the deck is unlocked. Crouching low, he pushes it open. The hinges screech horribly. A passing freight train, with its whistle blowing, would make less noise.

A long wait outside at the half-open door. Hann doesn't know who else is inside the cottage. If there is someone, they now know where Hann is.

There is nothing else to do. Hann quickly enters the cottage; turning right, he sees a tiny bedroom with a single window. Standing in the doorway, he realizes he is backlit by the light in the main room. Jumping to the other side of the door, Hann waits. Through the bedroom window, he sees his trooper with rifle raised. Hann lets out his breath and motions the fighter to come around. The trooper climbs up on the deck, starts through the open front door. Hann, without saying a word, signals him to stop.

Order given; Hann quickly looks around the main room. The dead man, at the table, lifeless eyes staring at a newspaper, the Daily Astorian. The man had finished his dinner before starting to read; a wine glass and plate pushed aside. Napkin and utensils on top of the dirty dinner plate. The table is large and seems to serve as a dining table, desk, and catch-all. In addition to the dinner items, there are books, mostly about birds, fishing tackle and other books, mostly about fishing. A pipe, tobacco pouch and lighter sit in an ashtray. On top of a stack of letters, a beautiful glass paperweight. Heavy, clear glass, with a swirl of brilliant blue in the center. For some reason, Herr Hahn picks it up and holds it in his hand.

All of this takes Obersturmbannfuhrer Hann less than a minute to take in.

At the opposite end of the main room; a doorway with no door, leads to a small kitchen. No light coming from it. Before moving to the kitchen, Hann reaches up and turns off the light above the table. Now, if there is an adversary, they would be on equal terms, both in the dark.

Hann stands beside the kitchen doorway; waiting for his heart rate to drop. Finally, he stretches his hand around the opening and throws the paperweight into the darkness.

The reaction is immediate.

"Jesus Christ, don't shoot me! Don't shoot." The shout, almost a scream, comes from the room.

Hann reaches around the kitchen doorway, feeling for a light switch. He finds it, turns the light on and spins through the door. Pistol pointed at the head of a tall, blond-haired man, who is shaking violently.

"Who are you? Tell me a lie and you will die." Hann says this in English.

"Jukka, I am Jukka."

"You only have one name?"

"I am Jukka Turpenen."

"What are you doing here, Jukka?"

"I am waiting for you."

With his pistol still pointed at Jukka's head, Hann said, "Do you have something to say to me, Jukka Turpenen?"

"Yes, they told me to say, Choke Point.

"Excellent, Jukka."

Jukka stared through the doorway at the dead man in the other room.

"I've never killed a man," Jukka says softly.

"Giese, bury the man at the table in back of the cottage," orders Hann.

"Yes, Sir. Should we bury Jukka also?"

"Not yet."

"Jukka, why did you think 12 boats and 24 men could stay in this tiny house?"

"This is a large property, you will see in the morning; there is a boathouse on the river 30 yards to the south, a barn upland from that and a bunkhouse 20 yards behind this cottage."

"Well done, Jukka."

"Thank you, Sir."

"Giese, have the rest of the property cleared and set up 4-corner guards, all hours, starting now."

"Yes, Sir."

PART 6

CHAPTER 21

"James Griffith, Astoria Country Club, calling for Colonel Daniel."

"Please hold."

Long moments of silence and several clicks later;

"Jim, good of you to call. What can I do for you?"

"Colonel, I'm calling regarding Lieutenant Newton . . . . Trigby."

"Yes, terrible business. Terrible."

"Well, yes, it is but Trigby's conduct has gotten out of hand."

"Good God, Jim, he's lost his wife and child, his . . . . his family."

"And we've given him allowance for that. But his behavior is affecting our members and staff. Accused the club president of cheating, in front of others. Slapped one of the caddies for giving him incorrect yardage. The yardage was correct."

"That is troubling, could___"

"Called me an 'over-the-hill buffoon,' masquerading as a golf pro. I won't tell you what he said about my wife."

"I will talk to him, Jim. Immediately."

"I'm sorry, Colonel, it's gone past that. We cannot have Lieutenant Newton on property again. The club will continue to offer no-cost memberships to all other officers at Fort Stevens, unless similar behavior occurs. If it does, all memberships, for all officers, will be revoked."

"I understand and will take care of this. I'm sorry for the mess, Jim."

"I'm sorry too, for Trigby. For now, he is not welcome or allowed here."

This is not the first incident of bad behavior from Trigby. And it won't be the last.

As an act of empathy for his loss, Trigby remains in the grand house off the parade grounds. This kind gesture makes things worse. He roams the house morning and night (he's given up on sleep), drinking directly from a bottle. For his rate of consumption, glasses and ice take too much time.

He hasn't unpacked any of the moving boxes. They sit in all the rooms, unopened, silent monuments to his loss. The kitchen is a wreck, even though he'd basically stopped eating. Trigby lost 20 pounds in the first 3 weeks. Officer's wives brought him food; casseroles, fried chicken – grief food. But Trigby, so often surly or drunk, the women stopped.

Both officers and enlisted covered for Lt. Newton out of respect for his family, his loss and the man he once was. That respect has begun to slip.

His uniform wrinkled, sometimes stained. Sick for more shifts than he works. Other doctors made sure he handled only the most basic of medical procedures when he did show up. Nurses wouldn't let him near the pharmacy locker.

Lieutenant Trigby Newton became a huge problem, the one everybody knew about and everyone prayed someone else would take care of.

The Medical Team at Fort Stevens will take part in a tactical war game. It will be a realistic response to an enemy (Japanese) attack on the Oregon coast. Specifically, Manzanita, Oregon, a sleepy beach town, 40 miles south of Fort Stevens. The units responding to the war game will not have warning.

"Why the hell would anybody invade Manzanita," is the enlisted reaction to this training program. But despite the grumbling, this will be a *real-time response drill*, which in plain English means every unit must take this drill seriously, or there will be consequences.

Colonel Daniel said it best at a command meeting of commissioned and non-commissioned officers; "Washington, at the highest level, will be watching us. I will accept nothing less than excellent results. If this standard is not met, there will be hell to pay, directly from me to you and your men."

This statement resonated with all present.

All Fort Stevens units; transport, artillery, infantry and medical, trained every day to be ready at a moment's notice; to mount up, head south and defend the coast. The medical unit's responsibility is to set up a Mobile Army Surgical Hospital and be ready to take in casualties.

Only a skeleton staff will remain on station at Fort Stevens. The depleted force could still repel an attack on the Fort, if one occurred, and could rely on reinforcements from the Forts across the River.

Trigby is a part of the Medical Team 'skeleton' force left behind during the drill. Fine with him. Realizing his drinking is a problem, he turned to beer during daylight hours. Easier to maintain an even strain with beer, as opposed to whiskey.

The surprise drill came on a Wednesday morning at 11AM. Fort Stevens emptied out like the Columbia River at low tide. Civilian traffic blocked on Highway 101, North and South, with Army vehicles strung out for miles on the road.

An orderly came to Trigby's house to inform him the drill is on and he could expect to be on duty for 2 or 3 days. Trigby had planned for this. A small valise held clothing, personal items, and another, 2 bottles of whisky and 6 beers. He knew he was short on the beer, but the bag wouldn't hold anymore. He could always come back to the house when he ran out.

His 'on duty' shift started immediately and would last until the drill is over. Trigby got to the medical quarters in good time, looking a little worse for wear but standing. He surveyed hospital areas, in-take and operating rooms. Said hello to all personnel and then retired to the on-duty officer quarters. He spent the early afternoon reclining on a cot, reading, sipping beer and now and again, a shot of whiskey.

Also on the skeleton crew is 1st Lieutenant, James Bidwell. Lt. Bidwell, handsome, dark-haired, popular with both officers and enlisted, secured 2 items that would surely make for an enjoyable Wednesday afternoon; a staff car and an off-duty nurse. The Lieutenant and nurse have been dating secretly for months. Fraternizing between officers and enlisted strictly forbidden and often overlooked. The nurse thinks it is turning into something serious; Lt. Bidwell (Jimbo to his friends) isn't so sure.

Jimbo is an outgoing, easygoing, likable officer; his father is the senior US Senator from Oregon. He could have received a light-duty posting in DC, but neither Lt. Bidwell nor the Senator wanted that. Both Bidwells served their country without fanfare or attention.

Almost empty due to the drill, the motor pool didn't have any vehicles except for Jeeps; not the transport Lt. Bidwell desired. Instead, he finagled a Major's staff car, left behind by an Officer participating in the drill.

The Lieutenant acquired a bottle of Rose and a picnic lunch from the Officer's Mess. He didn't demand or even ask for it; he merely inquired if 'picnic fixings' might be available. He is like that; people want to help him, whether they know of his father or not. A quality that serves him well.

With the blushing blond nurse in the passenger seat, Bidwell drove down to the Sunset Beach entrance. Windows down, the surf on one side, low beach dunes on the other and blue skies over both, they drive North on the beach, stopping at the wreck of the Peter Iredale for some photos.

The wreck of the Peter Iredale is one of the most visited spots on the Oregon coast. And has been for decades. 275 feet long, steel-hulled, with 4 masts, the Iredale was an impressive sailing ship. In the early hours of October 25, 1906, the ship was several miles off-shore, when a look-out spotted light from the Tillamook Rock Lighthouse.

The lighthouse does indeed sit on a rock, an acre of basalt. 1.2 miles off the coast, 20 miles South of the mouth of the Columbia. The rock rises 133 feet above the Pacific; the lighthouse built after blasting a level surface. 62 feet above the rock, the Tillamook Light shines seaward.

First lit in 1881, the light can be seen for 18 nautical miles. The welcoming light is a sign for ships to move closer to shore to meet the Columbia River Bar Pilot's boat. The Bar Pilot would take control of the vessel and guide it over the Bar, one of the most treacherous in the world.

As the Iredale moves up the coast, a strong on-shore wind came out of the North/Northwest, pinning the ship in the breakers. Several attempts at getting back into deep water failed. Wind, tide and darkness all joined forces to push the Peter Iredale hard into the beach. Hard enough to snap all four masts.

No lives were lost, no cargo was lost (the Iredale was sailing to Portland to secure a load of wheat for delivery to England). Another of the over 2,000 vessels wrecked trying to go over the Columbia River Bar, since the late 1700's. No wonder the area is known as the *'Graveyard of the Pacific.'*

Many parts of the Iredale salvaged, other parts looted and others worn down and washed away by time and tide. By the 1920's, there was still enough of the ship left to make it convenient for male beachgoers to change into bathing uniforms in the rusting interior.

Women were less inclined to use a communal, rusting, hulk of a ship to change into bathing apparel. Instead, they used hastily built '*cabanas*' that boyfriends or husbands would throw together, using material found on the beaches, mostly driftwood. Oregon beaches on the best days are windy and sometimes punctuated by these structures blowing away down the beach, with stunned females, clutching at whatever modesty they had left.

By the 1940's, the Peter Iredale still stands proud against the ravages of waves and wind. There is not enough left to use as a changing station, but the forecastle and bow still give a noble pose. But Lt. Bidwell and his date were seeking a more isolated picnic setting. They drove a ¼ mile more and parked away from the water, almost to the dunes.

A blanket laid on the sand, a wine bottle pinned down one end and the picnic basket holding down the other. Lt. Bidwell and his date sit in the lee of the parked staff car.

As Jimbo uncorked the wine, the idea of the staff car windbreak proves unwise. Lifting the bottle caused the blanket to flap like a banner. One of the glasses he'd set down blows 10 yards down the beach. Bidwell retrieved the glass, poured the wine, and found a ground-level sandstorm blowing into their filled glasses. They retreat to the staff car. When they lifted the picnic items off the blanket, it blew 20 yards down the beach, like a magic carpet. The Packard staff car went from a windbreak into a dining salon.

Finished with the picnic and half of the Rose, they drive South along the beach; laughing and sipping wine. The more they sip, the faster Jimbo drives. He demonstrates his driving ability with a figure 8, tires slipping and wine sloshing. It is fun at first, but after the 4th figure 8, his date is getting nauseous and wet from the spilled wine.

"Jimbo, Jimbo, slow down and turn around. That sign said we are in the Artillery Range."

"They're not firing today, with the drill on."

"To be on the safe side, turn around and slow down. My blouse is sopping wet."

"OK, just 1 more."

"Forward Watch Post 5 to Command."

"Command to Post 5, report."

"I've got a jackass driving erratically at a high rate of speed on the Artillery Range."

"Sending MP. Damn civilians, lucky for them, the Manzanita drill's on."

"That's the thing, Command; it's a staff car. Wait . . . Holy Shit . . . ."

"Report Post 5, Report."

"The car rolled over twice, maybe 3 times. Send an ambulance, send a couple. The passenger got thrown out the door like a rag doll. The driver hasn't come out; I think stuck in the car. This is bad; real bad, real stupid."

"Post 5, MP's 3 minutes out. Sending 2 ambulances, 12 minutes out."

"Command to Emergency Room. You have 2 ambulances inbound. Car crash, roll-over. Patients are 1 male, 1 female. Army personnel, 1 officer, 1 enlisted, both critical. Injury report; female, blood pressure, 100 over 60. Pulse 96, head trauma, possible broken shoulder and right arm. Male; low blood pressure, 65 over 35, elevated heart rate, 135, losing consciousness. Head trauma, complains of severe stomach and back pain."

"Roger, Command. ER ready."

The ER team suits up in cloth scrub dress, hats and masks, then moves to the operating room. The team has done this dozens of times; everyone knows their part and place. Charge Nurse Kathy Henderson, as her title indicates, oversees everybody but the Doctor. Kathy can be gracious and empathetic or no-nonsense and demanding, whatever the situation warrants. A large woman with a tangle of bright red hair, she can also show anger if needed. Those who see the anger never want to see it again.

The rest of the ER team consisted of an anesthesiologist, a scrub nurse, 2 floating nurses, and 2 medical corpsmen.

"Who's the Doc on duty?" This is from the anesthesiologist.

"Doctor Newton," Nurse Henderson replied.

"How is he?"

"Not sure; I'm waiting on him now.

Trigby is the last to show up. Dressed in scrubs, he enters the ER. He looks OK, not great, but presentable.

Nurse Henderson gives him the run-down.

"Arrival time, Kathy?"

"2 minutes, Doctor.

"Great, I'm ready!"

Was he ready? Nurse Henderson wondered. She could smell whiskey.

The ambulances arrive, patients off-loaded and rushed into the ER. At first glance, the male is the most seriously injured. He went into ER Operating Room #1. The female did have a nasty purple/yellow bump on her forehead, but neither arm nor shoulder are broken. Just badly bruised. She is held for observation.

"OK, let's get his clothes off and a saline drip going."

"Yes, Doctor."

Dr. Newton started his examination at the top of Lt. Bidwell's head. "I've got swelling on the back of the head, maybe a concussion. The gash on his forehead is bleeding like a son-of-a-bitch, but it's not deep. Apply a pressure bandage and I'll stitch it up later. Keep the blood out of his eyes. Oh, and his nose is broken. I'll set that later too."

Through this, Lt. Bidwell is in and out of consciousness, his eyes fluttering open and shut.

"Chest bruised, but ribs intact. Heavy swelling in the stomach; I'm not liking that. Hips and groin, OK. Right leg OK . . . . . and left leg OK. Nurse, check his feet."

"Did I miss anything, Kathy?"

"No, Doctor. I see it the same as you do. The bulge in the stomach is my main concern."

"Mine too. It could be a bunch of things. Internal bleeding, bowels, aneurysm, even the heart. Funny, no broken ribs."

"Doctor, I'm losing blood pressure; it's dropping like a stone. Heart rate sky-high. Whatever's wrong, we need to fix it now."

"Thank you, corpsman."

"Kathy, thoughts?"

"We could transport to Camp Adair in Corvallis; they have internal specialists."

"Hell, that'd take 3 hours. He's not gonna last that long. He'll die in route. Even if we operate here, now, his chances aren't great."

Bidwell is conscious long enough to hear that. He manages to raise an arm and whisper, "I don't want to die anywhere. Help me, dammit."

The decision is made. "OK then, here we go. Let's get him into surgery. Prep and drape. I'll scrub up."

Back in the surgery room, Trigby watched the anesthesiologist intubate the patient with an endo-tracheal tube down his throat, then attaching the tube to a ventilator.

As he watched, Trigby thought of stepping out for a moment to get a quick drink of whiskey, '*just to settle my nerves.*' He decides against it.

"Patient ready, Doctor."

"Give me vitals."

"Blood pressure low, but stable, 75 over 40. Heart rate still elevated, 130, but dropping."

"Scalpel."

The instrument slapped in Trigby's right hand, and his hand starts shaking. He can't control it. Has to use his left hand to steady his right. He looks up quickly. Everyone, watching him.

Trigby draws the scalpel down just below the ribs, through the skin, through muscle; when he breaches the abdominal cavity, blood explodes upwards. It covers the patient, the gurney and the team surrounding the patient. A nurse faints, the floor becomes slippery with blood; surgical gowns now red, covered in blood. Impossible to believe all this blood, coming from just 1 person. And it keeps coming.

'CLAMP! CLAMP! GIVE ME A CLAMP! Both of Trigby's hands are in the patient's stomach, hoping to staunch the blood. He knows the cause, a burst aortal aneurysm.

Lt. James Bidwell bled out in 45 seconds. Died on the table, under Dr. Newton's care.

CHAPTER 22

Trigby stood outside of Fort Steven's front gate. He's wearing civilian clothes because that's what he is. A civilian. Everything military has been taken away; his wartime over. He will never be welcome in any branch of military service. Nor any medical concern. Trigby cannot practice his profession anywhere a license is required.

After much discussion, angst and anger, it was decided the best thing for the Army and Senator Bidwell's son's memory would be a General Discharge for Lt. Trigby Newton. He certainly did not warrant an Honorable Discharge, and a General Discharge made an easier route for the Army and the Senator. No thought was given to Trigby's position. All concerned, just wanted him gone.

The Senator argued loud and long for Court Martial and Dishonorable Discharge. But that would mean a trial. A trial where facts would come out. Certainly, fraternization between 1st Lt. Birdwell and an enlisted nurse (actually, several nurses) would come up. And the fact Fort Stevens

Command was negligent in not placing Lt. Newton on family-distress sick leave after the death of his wife and son. Although Trigby had not caused Bridwell's death and most likely couldn't have saved his life, the ER staff should not have allowed Trigby to operate. And back to Fort Stevens Command, they were aware of Trigby's drinking and chose to ignore it.

Nobody would come out looking good in a Court Martial.

Trigby's medical license was removed by the Army and the state of Oregon. He could have challenged the 2 rulings but chose not to.

The nurse left Fort Stevens on a 30-day sick leave and then transferred to an Army Air Force base in Dodge City, Kansas. Trigby had all his household and personal belongings moved to a storage warehouse in Astoria and left Fort Stevens without saying goodbye to anyone. The medical staff at Fort Stevens, officers and enlisted, never mentioned Trigby's name again.

The only thing Trigby has, except for the clothes on his back, is money. The money from the sale of the Salem house. And the payment from the life insurance on his wife and child. In the only responsible move he could remember making in months, Trigby put the money in a safe deposit box at a bank in Astoria.

Trigby walked from Fort Stevens to the village of Hammond. He hitchhiked into Astoria, getting a ride with a trucker hauling fish.

"You look down and out, mister." The trucker says this with a cigar hanging from one side of his mouth. Ashes leaving a trail down the front of his jacket.

"Well . . . . I feel plain worn out."

"I hate to see someone looking like you. Maybe a shot of whiskey would help."

"Not sure about helping, but sure as hell wouldn't hurt. I'd be appreciative."

The trucker rolls down his window and spits a stream of tobacco juice. Most of it makes it out the window. Then he reaches under his seat and pulls out a whiskey bottle. Trigby recognizes the label as an old friend.

Pulling the cork out with his teeth, the grizzled road warrior, raised his right hand from the wheel and removed the cigar from his mouth. Driving with his knees, left hand holding the bottle and right hand his cigar, he takes a deep pull of whiskey. Passed the bottle to Trigby. Trigby lifted it to his mouth.

"That's a right long swallow you took from my bottle."

Trigby said, "and I thank you, it's a hard road I've been on."

The trucker left Trigby outside the Portway Tavern. Trigby started there and drank his way down the waterfront. Spent the night at a flop-house on Bond Street.

Trigby stayed in Astoria a while; he'd lost track of days, even weeks. They are all the same, a blur of drunken days and worse nights. On a cold, wet morning, Wes Layton, the minister of Astoria Christian Church, found Trigby Newton huddled on the church's steps. Pastor Layton knew of the deaths of Janet and Jamie Newton. The whole town did. The Pastor had thought he would perform the burial services; he wasn't asked, and there was no service.

The church geared up to help Trigby but he didn't want it. Pastor Layton hoped his appearance on the steps could be the start of a way back for Trigby Newton. He was wrong.

The Pastor got Trigby to his feet and drug him up to the entrance. With one arm wrapped around Trigby, he struggles to unlock the door. Trigby's legs seem to be unable to support his body. The door finally opens and the Pastor unloads Trigby's dead weight on the chair nearest the door. Trigby's eyes do not open. Pastor Layton ran down to the church kitchen to make coffee. Black and plenty of it.

15 minutes later, Layton returns with a coffee pot in one hand, a mug in the other. He sat both on the floor and shook Trigby. Shook him hard, no reaction. Pastor goes to the janitor's room, finds a pail and fills it with cold water. Empties it on Trigby's head.

Trigby awoke, startled. '*Where am I? Why am I wet?'*

The Pastor comes back with the bucket refilled. Dumps it over Trigby's head.

"WHAT THE HELL ARE YOU DOING? TRYING TO DROWN ME?"

"No, trying to sober you up. And then I'll probably have to delouse you. Next, I'll see to some proper clothing. My question to you, Trigby Newton, is what the hell are you doing to yourself."

"I'm fine just the way I am, dammit."

"Dammit to you. Is this the way you honor your family?"

"Leave my dead family out of this." Trigby, beginning to shake.

"Let's get some coffee in you and get you warm. We can go back to cussing then."

Pastor Layton bent down and filled the mug with coffee. Hands it to Trigby. In his office, the Pastor gets his Pendleton blanket he uses for afternoon naps.

Trigby has to double-fist the mug; got some coffee in his mouth, spilled most of it. It revives him and the blanket helps calm the shakes.

"I know where I am and why I came," Trigby's voice, slow but not slurred.

"I'm glad you came, son. Faith can be ___"

"I came to damn your faith. Your faith killed my family. My wife . . . . my son."

Pastor Layton didn't reply.

"And damn you and your faith. And damn God."

Trigby, standing now, blanket shrugged off, coffee pot kicked over. He felt like hitting the Pastor but doesn't. Struggles to open the glass-paned entrance door. Finally got it open and on his way out, punches his fist through one of the panels.

Pastor Layton watched Trigby stumble down the hill, heading for downtown. That is the last he would see of him. After a moment, Wes Layton kneels in front of the chair Trigby had been sitting on. Kneels in the coffee mess, his favorite blanket, a gift from his wife, soaked with coffee. He prays for Trigby and his lost soul.

Trigby took to sleeping nights outside at Lovell's Used Car lot at 13th and Duane, until he almost got run over by an exuberant car salesman with a cash customer. The brush with death took a toll on Trigby's morning. Luckily, he had a half-finished pint of peach brandy. The brandy went down quickly.

Sometimes trash cans are impossible to find. Trigby is a drunk, by anyone's measure, but not a person that litters.

Finally, at 14th and Commercial, a trash can. A satisfying thunk as the pint bottle hit the bottom of the can. He looks up, surprised to see the Astor Hotel across the street. Even more surprised to see an elephant, yes, an elephant being led out the hotel's front door.

Surprised isn't the right word. Bewildered, astonished, dazed, confused; none of these work either. It is as if the elephant stepped on Trigby's brain. Flattened it. Nothing made sense; reason has left the world. Steadying himself on the trash can, Trigby tries to make something of what his lying eyes are seeing.

Slowly a thought bubbled up.

'If this is real, what next, pigs that fly?'

Then another thought. Trigby tried to catch it but the idea flew out of his head. And then it came back;

'I have to stop drinking; I have to stop drinking.' And then a terrifying 3rd thought.

'Can I stop drinking?'

The pachyderm had been led inside the hotel and made a triumphant circle of the hotel's lobby. Now outside on the sidewalk, it slowly walks up a heavy ramp to the back of a flat-bed trailer and is lashed down tightly. The event was broadcast on the radio and most of Astoria came to see the spectacle. Day drinkers at the Fur Trader bar in the hotel lobby emerge from the dark bar, look at the pachyderm and head back into the bar. The driver towing the trailer has a loudspeaker:

"GREETINGS ASTORIANS, THE WAGNER GRAND 3 RING CIRCUS EXTRAVAGANZA WILL HAVE 7 0'CLOCK EVENING PERFORMANCES UNDER THE BIG TOP THURSDAY, FRIDAY, SATURDAY AND SUNDAY. WITH MATINEES ON SATURDAY AND SUNDAY AT NOON.

"DON'T MISS THESE SHOWS AND DON'T MISS THE MID-WAY. THRILLS, CHILLS AND EXCELLENT FOOD."

With an escort of 2 motorcycle cops in front and 2 squad cars in back, the trailer moves down Commercial Street to the county fairgrounds, the loudspeaker repeating the message. Moving slowly (with a 14,000-pound elephant, 13 feet high at the shoulder on a flat-bed trailer, speed is never a good idea), Trigby follows the procession easily on foot. As if the elephant has the answers to his sorrows.

His addiction, like an old friend, comes back to Trigby. At a liquor store along the way, he buys a bottle of vodka. Just the thought of peach brandy makes him nauseous.

Trigby watches the circus set up all afternoon. Gets kicked off the grounds a couple of times but gets back on with the offer of shared vodka. Didn't see the elephant up close until the evening. Caught sight of several elephants at the back of the fairgrounds. Trigby snuck down to see them, he has to see them.

It turns out there are 6 elephants in the show, a bull, 4 cows and a calf. The calf, 250 pounds at birth, now at 8 months; is a formidable, scary size. The others, so large they don't seem real and, as a result, are less frightening. Trigby watches from a distance; this is their feeding time. Adult elephants eat 495 pounds of food, mostly hay, every day. Their feeding time is any time they are not performing or sleeping.

Trigby is drawn to them; can't help himself. As he gets nearer and nearer, the elephants do not stop eating; they know people and this person is meek, almost invisible. Very close now, Trigby is mesmerized. As they eat, the elephants sway back and forth. Back and forth, in unison! Trigby needs to be a part of this (the vodka is pretty much gone).

Being near the bull does not seem a good idea. The bull is the biggest creature in a group of outstandingly big creatures. Standing close to the calf or its mother is another non-starter. Trigby chose to stand between 2 of the cows. The sheer size of them, the fecund, humid smell of them. Their dusty, rough skin, almost sharp. He can hear their breathing.

And the swaying. Constant, comforting, welcoming. Trigby is at the widest part of the 2 cows. Their stomachs? They must sense him; he is not crushed. He is with them, in the swaying. Calming, soothing. Trigby falls asleep, standing up.

"What the hell are you doing down there? God dammit, get up."

Does the man have a hammer? No, a cane that he uses to beat Trigby, holding the back of his coat to raise Trigby halfway up.

"Get up, you bastard, get up. Wonder you didn't get killed. How stupid are you, sleeping under a bunch of elephants?" A blow from the cane accompanies each word.

Amazingly Trigby's mind is somewhat clear. *'If you want me to stand up, why are you hitting me? Stop it and I'll get up.'* Trigby thought this but didn't say it. Or the next thought. *'How old is this guy? Why don't I take his cane and start beating him?'* He reached up and grabbed the cane. Used it to get to his feet.

"I was a damn good batter in, in, in (Trigby couldn't find the word, finally, it comes) college. Bet I could hit your head off your shoulders." The watchman backed up, Trigby swinging the man's cane in a vicious, clumsy manner. "I'm up and out of here, you old, dried-up raisin."

'Dried-up raisin?' Even Trigby can't figure out where that came from. He walks toward downtown, turns and walks back to the cowering, defenseless watchman. "Here's your cane, didn't want you to think I'm a thief."

Trigby stopped by to see the elephants a couple of nights; when he came back on Monday, the circus is gone.

CHAPTER 23

Without a family, profession, or hope, Trigby has no particular place to go. Without a thought, he heads across the River. The ferry, Tourist III, berthed at the foot of 14th Street, takes him across the Columbia. The bright day and wind sobers Trigby. He sits outside on a hard wooden bench.

Trigby fell asleep on the way to Megler on the Washington side of the Columbia. He stayed asleep for the return trip. Wakes up when the ferry bangs into the pilings alongside the dock at Astoria. Trigby rouses himself and walks up the passenger dock. Seeing the Astoria Hotel confuses him.

He finally figures it out, gets back on board the ferry and reclaims his bench. Trigby slept on the bench for 2 more round-trips and would have stayed there forever if not for the Captain of the ferry.

Captain Smith noticed the sleeping bum as he went down to the coffee shop for a refill. The ferry docked at Megler, cars unloading first and then the walkers going ashore. Smith nudged the man with the toe of his boot, he didn't want to touch him. No response. Again, with the boot, still no response. The 3rd try, almost a kick, gets the man's attention.

"Time to get off your ass and off my ferry." Captain Smith runs a tight ship, with no place for a vagrant. "Move it, now." He doesn't recognize the bum as his friend from the country club. Trigby, now awake, knows who is kicking him. Trigby mumbles, "you couldn't hit a 3 iron if your life depended on it."

Captain Smith wondered about the golf reference as he watched the bum stumble down the steps to the main deck and then up the '*Walkers Only*' ramp to shore.

Trigby stands onshore at the ferry landing in Megler, looking at a road sign. Under an arrow that points West; Chinook, Ilwaco, Long Beach, Naselle. Too many towns, too many people. At the bottom of the sign, an arrow pointing East, Quarantine Station - 2 miles.

Those are his choices. He heads East.

It takes 2 miles for Trig to be exhausted. Just up ahead, the Quarantine Station. They have an extra cot. In the morning, after a shower, coffee and toast, Trigby is back on the road. Got a ride from a farmer, headed to Naselle.

He had room up front but made Trigby ride in the back of the pickup.

Trigby stays a while in Naselle. He sleeps rough under a picnic table at the town park. There is a road-side motel, but they won't rent him a room; even after he's shown them he has money. He spends his days in the public library, catching up on the news and napping. For food, he eats in the alley behind the Koffee Kup Kafe. He pays for the food, but they don't let him eat inside. The dishwasher at the KKK befriended Trigby and gave him a blanket and a bottle of whiskey. When the whiskey ran out, Trigby bought a gallon of Tokay wine. His friend gave him a coffee cup because it's hard to drink from a gallon jug.

Trigby is fine with staying in Naselle and probably dying there. He really didn't care but the police moved him on. "We'll give you a ride 2 miles east of town. Don't come back." He didn't.

He continues East; he's stopped trying to get a ride. Walks with the gallon of Tokay, sipping from it, losing a lot in the process. At night or when Trigby gets *'too damn tired,'* he steps off the roadway and sleeps.

Trigby walks through the villages of Grays River and Rosburg. Could have stopped but keeps going. One foot in front of the other, no thoughts in his mind. He should have stopped in Rosburg. The road begins to climb; it wears Trigby out. He thinks of lying on the white center line and going to sleep. Finally gets to the top of the highlands, can't remember how long it took him to get there. It turns out the descent is worse, harder on his knees. He stumbles into the town of Skamokawa.

And that's where he stayed. Never really decided to stay; just couldn't go any farther. He found a room in a boarding house that catered to cannery workers, cash in advance. Trigby, looked into the mirror in his room, *'if they rent to me, they'll rent to anybody.'*

What appealed to Trigby isn't the boarding house itself; bed too soft, food not great, but the location, perfect. Next to a low-down bar and sometimes grill. Doug's Bar isn't much; in fact, it barely stands upright. Inside, the only source of light and décor are beer signs. The bar itself, a door laid over sawhorses, the grill, a hot plate.

Trigby arrives at Doug's the moment it opens at 7am and stays until it closes. As the day wears on and the alcohol level increases to dangerous levels, Trig gets agitated and argumentative. Ranting about his hatred for God and religion, or anything else that displeases him. And everything and everybody displeases him.

But he is a regular at the bar and, more importantly, a regular source of cash flow. His behavior overlooked, at first. After a while, Trigby became an annoyance to everyone at the bar and finally a nuisance. When he gets 86'd from the worse bar in the world, even Trigby realizes things need to change.

CHAPTER 24

Missing Doug's Bar as his daily rendezvous with humanity, Trigby takes to setting outside Skamokawa's only grocery store. On a rainy day, he'd sit on a bench under the awning at the front of the store. On a sunny day, he sits on the side of the store, no awning, soaking up the sun. Trigby developed a 'farmers tan'; brown forehead, sunburnt cheeks and hands. The rest of his body; shockingly white.

The grocery became Trigby's new source of alcohol; gallon jugs of Tokay. But he saved that for his room at the boarding house. The thought of sitting outside a retail establishment sipping from a gallon jug of wine embarrassed even Trigby. He kept a pint of whiskey in his jacket pocket. The new surroundings cut his intake of booze.

"That bright sun is sure welcome, isn't it? You look right comfortable; mind if I join you?"

No response from Trigby; he's given up talking to people.

"I'll take that as a yes." The man dark-haired, middle-aged, a bit roly-poly. "Yes sir, it's nice an warm right here!"

No response from Trigby.

The 2 men sat there, not talking, watching passers go by, enjoying the sun on their faces.

"Good looking bunch of apples in the store; I got 6. Bought apples last week, all of them mealy. Hope these are better. Want an apple?"

Something missing at the boarding house is fresh fruit. Or fresh anything, for that matter.

"Sure, I'll take one," Trigby muttered. It's the most he'd said to anyone in a week.

"Here you go then."

Neither spoke until the apples were gone.

"Thank you."

"You're welcome."

And that's how it started. That man and that apple started Trigby out of the hole he'd dug for himself. He started to get his life back. Not all the way, not even close. Heartsick, diminished, he made small steps back into the world and out of the bottle.

The men didn't introduce themselves, just chatted. War news, weather, sports, the things men talk about. Each had another apple.

"Well, I best be going home. Is that jacket warm enough for you? Cold weather coming in tomorrow."

"It's a raincoat."

"OK, is that raincoat warm enough? I've got a coat that's getting too darn tight for me, should fit you."

Part of the reason, a small part, Trigby drank is to stay warm. "I could use a little warmth."

"Great, I live up the hill, behind the Church. Come an__"

"No thanks, Churches and I don't agree."

"Well, a jacket doesn't have any religious significance; it just keeps you warm."

"I hate religion."

"There are times I do too. But listen, I'll leave the jacket outside on the porch for a couple of days. Come get it if you change your mind. Good talking to you."

Cold weather did come the next day. The day after that, Trigby hiked up the hill, marched past the sign that said **Peace Lutheran, Everett Lawson, Pastor** and came to a blessed halt at a small house. The steep climb had cost Trigby. Sweating, heart pounding, lungs complaining. *'I am so out of shape.'*

A stout, middle-aged woman, at the side of the house, beating a rug, slung over the clothesline with a broom.

"I've come for the jacket." Trigby hollered, louder than necessary.

"What?"

"The jacket. I want it."

"I'll get Everett." She put down the broom.

"Can I just get the jacket?"

"Well, I didn't think that jacket should sit out on the porch, night after night. It's inside; I'll get it and get Everett." She says this in a no-nonsense tone of voice. Direct, but not unfriendly.

She went inside and didn't come back for a good while.

'Well, how long do I have to wait for the damn jacket?' Trigby thought this, but he stayed. Picked up the broom and started beating the rug. Ducked under the clothesline and beat the other side. It felt oddly enjoyable. Trigby started to work up a sweat, began hitting harder. Hit the rug like he had a baseball bat in his hands. Next, a golf swing for the lower part of the rug.

Everett Lawson and his wife, Helen, stood on the porch watching Trigby.

"Just wanted the dust out of that rug. Didn't want it dead!" Everett's voice rang out.

"Sorry," Trigby put the broom down. "I kinda got into it."

"Great, here's the coat I was talking about."

"Thank you."

"You're welcome. I'm Everett Lawson and this is my wife, Helen. Our daughter Jenny is too shy to come out."

Trigby shook hands with both. "I'm Trigby Newton and I guess I should get going."

"Hope you put the coat to good use," Everett replied.

"Wait boys, wait. That jacket is worth more than a thank you. Trigby, you were good with that rug; I have 2 more inside. Please help me carry them out and you can have a go at them."

"Yes, Ma'm."

A couple of days later, Everett saw Trigby at the grocery store.

"Helen wants some furniture moved. She's repainting the living room that got repainted 2 years ago. Will you help her? We can pay." Everett Lawson didn't get his rotund figure by physical labor. He got it by avoiding all things physical, particularly labor.

"I don't need money."

"OK, Trigby, just thought I'd ask."

"I do need something to do. I'll move the furniture and repaint the room."

"Well, thank you, Trigby!"

"Glad to help."

The parsonage is the lowest rung of all Church property, the last to get maintenance, remodeling, improvement. An unwritten rule insists the parsonage is the parson's responsibility. It is his family's home, after all, and a no-rent home to boot!

At Peace Lutheran, the parsonage is a modest, rectangular, 2-story house. It sits up the hill from the church, up from the parking lot, past a small baseball field and a neat front yard. A person visiting leaves their automobile in the parking lot and hikes up, past the baseball diamond, through the usually wet front yard, to a level patch the blue-shingled house sits on. A well-maintained garden borders the long front side of the home.

This is a problem for new visitors; there seems to be no way to enter. A large picture window and 2 smaller windows, no door. After a pause to ease lungs, a new visitor usually heads left through the garden, turns right at the corner of the house in search of the front door. The search is in vain; no door on this short side of the house. The visitor now heads along the back of the house, still no entry. Several windows on this side but no door. Turning at the corner of the house, a short set of steps can be seen, leading to a small overhang landing and, finally, the front door.

At this point, most people think and some say, *'thought I'd have to climb through a window to see the Pastor.'*

Through the front door is a small, narrow room, the mud room. Coats on hooks and shoes underneath. Barely enough room to take your coat off and no place to sit when you kick your shoes off. Past that, to the left, is a good size living room, used only for guests. Straight ahead of the mud room is a pleasant dining room. This room contains Helen's pride and joy, a 'dining room ensemble.' Sideboard, hutch, expandable table that seats 8; 12 in a pinch, and 8 matching chairs.

On the left side of the dining room is a wall with 2 doors; 1 to the Everett's bedroom and 1 to the only bathroom. Through double doors at the far end of the living room is the largest room in the house, the kitchen.

The kitchen is the center of all activity in the household. And it is Helen's territory, all of it. You are welcome if you remain seated and out of the way.

Painted a light blue, the room is a bright, open space. The newest appliance is an icebox with compressor on top. The oldest appliance is the GE stove; it looks like it comes from another age. Helen is thankful for the large, one-piece sink with a draining area on the side. A large window above the sink looks out to the forest behind the house.

Checkerboard linoleum is the functional flooring; Helen hates it. The meanest part of the kitchen is the ironing board inset into the wall. When Jenny was younger and more inquisitive, she opened the door just to see what was inside. The heavy board fell out on the top of her head.

The strangest thing in the kitchen is an exposed stairway on the back wall, leading to the 2nd floor. Steps jut out from the wall, with no railing. If you stumbled and fell, you'd land on top of the icebox.

The kitchen is Helen's domain and the upstairs is Jenny's. There isn't a door at the top of the stairs; you are immediately in Jenny's bedroom. Bed, dresser, clothing hanging on a pipe, no closet. It is a good-sized room and through a door is another equally large room. This is the *Toy Room.*

All parts of Helen Lawson's home are neat, clean and 'picked up.' The only exception is the Toy Room. Here nothing is picked up; toys everywhere. They can be left on the floor for days, maybe months. Dolls and their clothes scattered about, no neatness in the Toy Room. Helen makes herself go in every 6 months, just to tidy up.

Trigby moved furniture out of the Lawson's living room. Helen is particular about how the painting proceeds. She will do the painting herself, but Trigby can help. Moving tarps, cleaning brushes, that sort of thing. Helen started with the woodwork, took an hour to do 1 short side of the room. She is a fussy painter but not a neat one. Paint smudges on the wall, on the wood floor, rug. And herself.

"You look like a survivor of an artillery attack, using paint."

"Thank you for your support, Trigby. I suppose you want to try?"

"Yes, Ma'm." Trigby painted the remaining woodwork in an hour and a half. Came back the next day to do the walls. Came back the day after that and replaced the furniture. The next week he repainted the Lawson's dining room.

Trigby wouldn't accept money but would accept food. Home-cooked food. The routine became; Trigby works, Helen cooks, and Everett disappears into the Church, coming back for lunch and reappearing an hour before dinner.

"Mrs. Lawson, you aren't much of a painter, but you are one hell of a cook!"

"Hell has nothing to do with it, Trigby; my Mother taught me."

Trigby becomes a regular visitor to the Lawson household. The hard part for Trigby is the Lawson's 6-year-old daughter, Jenny. Hard for Trigby to be around people, extremely hard to be around children. Jenny's shyness makes it easy for her to be ignored, to blend into the background. A 6-year-old wallflower.

The more Trigby worked around the house and Church, Jenny became harder to ignore. *'Hell, she's just a kid; what am I blaming her for? When'd I get so rude?'* Trigby got over his discomfort with the child by treating her like an adult.

Jenny, with her quiet style, is nice to be around. A serious child, black hair, with wide dark brown eyes, glasses and a 'page-boy' haircut, she becomes Trigby's aide-de-camp. The friendship bloomed with after-dinner card games. Jenny taught Trigby how to play Fish; he didn't tell her he'd played it before. Trigby taught Jenny how to play 21.

"Trigby, I hardly think that is an appropriate pastime for a 6-year-old."

"I like it, Mom. Hit me, Trigby!"

Helen and Everett noticed the friendship and approved of it. Jenny, the only child Trigby could be near, but it's a start.

The children's room at the Church needed painting. Trigby chose Jenny to be his painting assistant. He refused payment but made sure his assistant got .10 cents an hour. Jenny decided on the color for the room, a screaming orange.

"I gotta wear sunglasses to paint this."

"I like it! Let's get going." Jenny's white painter's hat kept slipping down over her glasses.

"She'll make a huge mess, Trigby." Helen had come to check on the painting party.

"Less of a mess than you, Mrs. Lawson."

"I can poison your plate at dinner, Trigby."

"And who would do the chores? Everett?"

Mrs. Lawson, her daughter, and Trigby, all laughed.

CHAPTER 25

Sunday Dinner

"Wow, it sure smells good here, Mrs. Lawson." Trigby finished cutting the lawn around the cottage and Church.

"Thanks, Trigby; come in and wash up. Dinner's ready in 15 minutes. And take your shoes off. You're tracking grass all over my clean floor."

"Yes, Ma'am."

The chicken dinner, unusual during war-time rationing. The chicken made it unusual; strictly rationed, the bird on Lawson's table came from a congregation member's farm. Canned corn and peas, mashed potatoes and bread made up the rest of the meal.

"Mom, these pink potatoes are funny looking!"

"I agree," Trigby seconded.

"Well, if you could get me real butter instead of oleomargarine, they would look normal." Butter, rationed to near extinction, had been replaced by oleo, a corn-based spread.

"Jenny, I told you before, its pink because the dairy farmers want to ensure you don't think it's butter."

"Everett, don't talk with your mouth full."

"Yes, dear."

"We could mix it yellow with food coloring," Jenny again.

"I agree," Trigby again.

"Both of you stay out of my food coloring."

"Yes, M'am!" Trigby winked at Jenny as he said it.

She winked back.

Tuesday Dinner

"Trigby, you say you have money?" Helen Lawson asks this at the dinner table. Dinner is Spam on toast, with canned corn and peas for dinner. Canned peaches for dessert.

"I do."

"How much?"

"Enough."

"Enough to buy some decent clothing?"

"I guess."

"Well, buy some. Your elbow's coming through the sleeve of the shirt you're wearing. The shirt you've been wearing for as long as we've known you."

"I don't buy clothes, my wif___."

"OK, not that I don't have enough to do; but I'll help get you some clothes."

"I'm not sure of my sizes anymore, Mrs. Lawson."

"Listen, Trigby, you're coming along, Jenny and I will pick them out; you'll try them on and pay for them."

That Saturday, Trigby and the Lawson family drove to Megler and took the ferry to Astoria. Banking and spending for Trigby, fashion direction for Helen and Jenny. The Pastor headed for one of the many Lutheran Churches in Astoria for a bit of pastoral fellowship.

Trigby dug money out of his safe deposit and meekly followed the girls to Burke's Men's store. Shoes, socks, belt, wallet, underwear, casual pants, casual shirts, dress slacks, dress shirt and a navy blazer with brass buttons.

"Are you kidding me, Mrs. Lawson? What do I need this for?"

"Well, Trigby, you might want to take a lady out to dinner." She was sorry, the minute she said it.

Weighed down with packages, Mrs. Lawson, Trigby and Jenny made it to the car just as Everett walked up.

"Can I help?"

"Not now, dear. 5 blocks ago, yes, you could have helped. Not now."

The Lawsons were ready to catch the ferry and head home. Trigby insisted they take a later ferry and have dinner at Theil Brothers. "My treat!"

As they walked by the bar at the restaurant, Trigby realized he hadn't had a drink in weeks.

Dinner the next day; tuna, noodle and pea casserole. Chocolate cake for dessert.

Helen demanded Trigby wear his new clothes. "Now that you're dressed like a decent citizen, it's time we got you decent housing."

"Thanks, Mrs. Lawson; I'm OK with where I'm at."

"It's a hellhole, but we have a solution. There is a room in the basement of the Church. It has a shower, toilet, and a hot plate. Bed and bureau, and a window. It was used when the Church had traveling ministers, didn't have a full-time minister."

"It'd be fun!" said Jenny. And the decision is made.

Jenny and Trigby painted the basement room. This time, Jenny chose a pastel yellow for the walls and white for the woodwork. It brightened the room up.

There is a condition for the room and what amounted to Trig's board at the Lawson's dinner table. No booze. Trigby agreed and stuck to it.

Trigby didn't attend Church services, still not comfortable around people. But he did listen to Sunday sermons lying on his bed in the basement room. And it helped. Trigby kept up repairs on the cottage and Church. If a churchgoer needed a door hung or a pipe snaked, Trigby is the go-to guy. A cow calving, he helps the local vet. The vet, along with the pastor, are the only 2 people who know Trigby's story. Everybody else knows him as an OK, quiet man.

There is a sense of sorrow about Trigby that is noticed but not commented on.

PART 7

CHAPTER 26

"Come on, Sandy, time for school."

The golden retriever bounds out the farmhouse's front door, runs across the porch, takes the front steps in a single leap and sits, tail wagging, at the passenger door of the Ford pick-up.

Sandy loves school.

Sally opens the truck door. "Get in." Sandy leaps up to her seat inside the truck.

Sandy's owner walks around the truck, opens the driver's door and climbs in. She adjusts the rear-view mirror, says a prayer for the '*damn old truck' to* start. Prayer answered, Sally Mather drives to her job at the Lincoln Elementary School in Grays River, Washington. Sally teaches 2nd grade.

"Hello, Miss Mather."

"Good morning, Molly."

"I put a cup of coffee and a roll on your desk and a treat for Sandy."

"You do spoil us, Molly. Thank you."

With Sandy right behind her, Miss Mather opens the door to her classroom. Tall windows running the length of the class make the small room seem larger. Sally raised the window blinds that had been lowered for yesterday's afternoon sunshine. The room smells of books, chalk and the dust of 60 years of schooling Grays River's youth.

At her large, wooden desk in front of the blackboard, Sally drank her coffee and ate the roll. She glanced at her daily lesson plan; the principal required each teacher to submit their plan every Monday. She set the plan aside and dismissed it from her mind. Sally saw teaching 2nd grade as a boxing match. *'Plan all you want, but when the 1st punch gets thrown, the plan hits the floor.'* Sally's idea is to get down with the kids, see them at eye level and go nuts! She made her voice loud, her movements big. Get the kids to see school as fun. Make every school day the best school day in her student's lives.

Sandy, her treat, 2 meatballs from Molly's dinner the night before, gone in an instant. With her nose, she nudges at her empty water dish and looks at Sally. No reaction. Nudges again and licks Sally's ankle.

The shock causes Sally to bang her knees on the bottom of the desk's center drawer. "Gracious, Sandy, I'll get your water. Who runs this show, you or me?"

They both know Sandy runs the show.

Watered and fed, Sandy plodded to her station at the back of the classroom. Rather than lay down slowly, she collapses with a loud thud. Front and back legs splayed out. Lying on her stomach, watching the door, eyes half-closed.

The official start time at Lincoln Elementary is 9AM. Students wait outside; some play schoolyard games, kickball, basketball, tetherball and any other physical activity that wears kids out. Other students work feverishly on homework they should have done last night. And others, not many, sit by themselves, wanting to be a part of things, but knowing they won't.

When the 9 o'clock bell rings, the kids roar into school. Miss Mather's 2nd graders all stop to greet Sandy. The dog stands for the students and regally allows herself to be petted. When that is over, she plops down again and promptly goes to sleep with a soft snore. The next time she gets up will be recess, the favorite part of her day.

The only exception to this routine is the rare occasion when Miss Mather must get an unruly student back under control. Immediately Sandy is wide awake, sitting at attention, staring at the misbehaving student. With order restored, Sandy flops on the floor and falls asleep in minutes.

At the front of the classroom, across the top of the blackboard, is the alphabet in cursive. Facing the board and Miss Mather, the class can see a picture of President Roosevelt on the right and the American flag on the left.

"Students, today is going to be a great day! Does everybody agree with me?"

"Yes, Miss Mather."

"Good; let's start this great day by pledging our allegiance to the United States of America."

At noon recess, Sandy played, or more accurately, interfered in every schoolyard game. Sally uses lunch and recess time as a welcome relief. She eats a light lunch alone, needing quiet; the noon break is like a spell between rounds. And then the bell rings and the next round starts.

4PM the same day.

"Sandy, let's go home; I'm bushed." The dog spent the afternoon dozing and now seems spry, dancing beside Sally as they walk to the truck. When they arrive home, Sandy examines the yard, barn and field for any irregularities. Finding none, she lays on the porch surveying her realm.

Sally opens the screen, unlocks the front door, lets the screen door slam against the door frame. The farmhouse, stuffy and quiet, Sally opening windows. This time of day, Sally feels loneliness, like a bad dream, barely remembered. The house is silent, the only living thing she can talk to, can't respond.

Turning the radio on helps. Sally is addicted to music of all kinds. But only good music. She hums along with the tunes as she cooks dinner. Chicken soup with dumplings, the chicken from her farm.

Sally refers to her age as mid-30's and wonders when late-30's begins. With brown hair in a 'sensible' cut and beautiful hazel eye, she is a tall woman who stands up straight. Cheerful and winsome, with a bit of sorrow, well hidden.

There have been men in Sally's life, for sure. Not many and few recently. Was Tim, her first love, the love of her life? She isn't sure and her life isn't even close to being over. Tim and Sally were classmates first, then friends, then boyfriend/girlfriend and their senior year of high school, soul mates.

Sally and Tim were the odd teenagers in love that planned. Planned their future, planned their lives. College first, then marriage. Both applied to state colleges, Washington State in Pullman and University of Washington in Seattle. Tim, an all-state 1st team in football, had been scouted and offered scholarships by both. Michigan State also promised Tim a scholarship.

"Son, it's as plain as this; Michigan State is a hell of a lot better known than Washington State or UW. There is a great program at Michigan State, a nationally known program. Hardly anybody outside the West Coast knows or cares about Washington schools."

"George, stop it. Honey, your father wants to ship you off to Michigan to continue his family's tradition of Michigan State graduates. His father went to Lansing, so did his grandfather and so did he. If he has his way, we'll all move to Lansing."

"Martha, this is a helluva chance for our boy. Out of state, full-ride scholarship to Michigan State. You don't turn down this kind of opportunity. If he does well, and we know he will, he could even turn pro."

"And join a gang of toothless ruffians, beating each other up? Is that what you want for our only child?"

"It's a goo___"

"I'm fine with either Washington school, although I'd prefer the one in Seattle, it's closer and I could find some decent shopping."

"Listen to me, Ti___. Where the hell did he go?"

Neither parent noticed their son slip away. Tim headed for Sally's house. They spent the evening on a porch swing, under the watchful eyes of her parents. Tim hated to admit it, but he agreed with his father. But didn't want to be away from Sally. Tim knew his potential would be in football, but when he looks at her, he knows Sally is his future.

Eventually, Tim chose Michigan State.

Sally went to Longview, Washington Community College. She was heartsick about Tim's decision and, at the same time, wanted the best for him. Loved him that much. She was torn about being part of this real-life fairy tale. A small-town kid with the big arm wins the big prize; a 4-year free ride to a major school. But Sally, the girlfriend, the soulmate, stays home.

Tim knew how she felt; they talked about it constantly. They would get through the separation, would see each other during school breaks. She would travel east; he would be home during the summer. The main thing, they were in love and they would work it out.

But they didn't work it out.

Tim is a big success in college. Starting quarterback his sophomore year. 4.0 student. He stayed on campus the first summer; then his parents moved from Grays River to Michigan. And the letters started arriving farther and farther apart. Finally dwindled to Christmas cards every few years.

Sally did see Tim once after he left college. A few years after graduation, he and his wife stopped in Grays River on their way to Seattle. Tim landed a good job; his wife, beautiful and pregnant. They were a handsome couple. Sally, glad for them both.

Sally got her teaching certificate and stayed in Grays River. She taught her 2nd-grade class and lived in a small apartment near school. First with a roommate and then alone.

Her parents had Sally when they were in their early 40's, unheard of at the time. As the years passed and her parent's health declined, Sally moved back to the family farm. That was a good time for the 3 of them. All got along and Sally felt she was paying them back for all they had given her.

Sally's father died first of a heart attack and 6 months later, her mother died of a broken heart.

And then Sally was alone. Lonely, but with her teaching and the farm to run, she stayed busy. And built a life for herself.

She had friends, both women and men. The women, mostly from school. The men, some friends from school, some acquaintances and a couple that were more serious. Including one from Astoria, who turned out to be married. She wondered why they always had to meet in Chinook.

After that experience, Sally bought herself a dog and named her Sandy. The dog, a golden retriever with a good nature and an independent streak a mile wide. They became inseparable, the dog's idea, not Sally's. They went everywhere together.

The only dispute between dog and master was the dog on furniture and bed. The dog for it, Sally against it. She made a beautiful dog bed for Sandy. The dog wouldn't go near it. Next, an expensive dog bed from the Sears catalog. The only time Sandy pee'd in the house was when she pee'd on the Sears dog bed. Finally, Sandy won and claimed her rightful place on the couch and at the end of Sally's bed.

Sally thought to herself, "I'd rather sleep with a 4-legged dog than a 2-legged one."

CHAPTER 27

"Sally, you know the big football game at the high school is on Friday an___"

"Jill, I'm not a sports fan."

"It's the big game against Naselle."

"Isn't that the team we've lost to for the past decade?"

"I thought you weren't a sports fan."

"I'm not, but it's such an amazing record."

"OK, listen, I need you to fill in for Madge Thomas with the cheerleading squad."

"No way!"

"It's just for this game. I would do it myself, but I'm running the snack stand. Madge is having root canal done on Friday and won't be in any condition to__"

"I'd trade her, straight up."

"Sally, I'm begging you. You just stand there and keep the cheerleaders away from the boys. Nothing to it."

"I teach at the grade school. You couldn't find anyone at the high school to help?"

"They all turned me down. I'd owe you big time."

"How big?"

"Sally, I'll give you my grandmother's recipe for rhubarb pie."

Sally had tasted the pie and was turned down when hinting about the recipe.

"OK, Jill, I'll do it. If . . . "

"Bless you."

"If I have the recipe by Friday morning."

"So little trust, Sally."

First off, Sally didn't like sports, particularly violent sports with unexplainable rules, like football. Second, she thought cheerleading, was a demeaning endeavor for young women. And lastly, Sally had tried out for her junior high cheer squad and wasn't chosen.

Friday night, a typical late October night, wet and miserable. Sally stands on the sidelines, shivering. She has on so many layers of clothing; she'd lost count. "Betsy, I don't want to tell you again, leave the players alone. You are on the cheer squad, not the football team." Between the catcalls from the boys in the stands and the cheerleaders primping for the players, Sally had had it with girls, boys, sports and hormones. If she ever did this again, she'd bring a gun.

Grays River had gained their losing record, honestly. They lacked good coaching and decent players, but the overall lack of team spirit or interest stood out the most. It appeared the players grew up hoping to be on a losing team. The gruff Grays River coach, Bill Wright won a coin toss bet; as the winner, he got to coach the football team for a year, the loser had to coach for 3 years.

Middle of the 1st quarter, Grays River behind 28 to zero; with a 3rd down, 27 yards for a 1st down. Grays River Coach Wright sent in the play with the fullback. "OK, Ricky 49 left sweep. Run like hell." As he ran to the huddle, Ricky stared at the cheer squad; at the end of the game, he'd ask the head cheerleader for a date. For the 5th time.

Ricky delivered the play to the quarterback wrong; "49 RIGHT sweep." The quarterback repeated the play "49 right sweep, on 3." With the ball on the right hash mark, the play makes no sense. To run right means the fullback will have little room to get around his linemen; he'd run out of bounds before he gains any yardage. Run the play to the left and ¾ of the field, wide open. One could hope a player on the Grays River team would realize the play is running the wrong way. One would be disappointed.

"Hut 1, hut 2, hut 3." The football snapped, quarterback hands off the ball to Ricky, the fullback, who joins the parade behind the pulling right guard and halfback running hard towards the end of the Grays Rivers offensive line. Before he can turn up field, Ricky is out of bounds, as are the rest of the players on both teams.

The pulling guard plows into a Grays River sophomore cheerleader knocking her to the ground. As she struggled to get up, the halfback hit her with a perfect cross-body block. This time she stays down. Even with the referees' whistles blowing at a screeching pitch, the players continued blocking, tackling everybody in sight.

Finally, order is restored! The sideline looks like a bomb site. Cheerleaders down, pompons strewn like poppies after a windstorm. Players down, some without helmets, some without shoes. The Naselle coach runs across the field, screaming at his players to get up and get back on the field. Coach Wright screaming at his players for running the "wrong goddam way, are you all crazy?" Time out called. The 49-sweep to the ~~left~~/right lost 2 yards.

Sally didn't see any of it coming. She is standing on the sidelines, chastising a cheerleader for flirting with her leering boyfriend in the stands. She heard the unmistakable sound of a body hitting another body at high speed. As she turned to the sound, the Grays River right tackle hit her with a shoulder block. The tackle (the biggest player on the team) tried to stop but couldn't.

The pain instantaneously went through Sally like an electrical current. She is falling now, driven by the tackle's forward motion and weight. When she hit the ground, there are 2 more blows, the ground and the tackle landing on top of her. Her breath left with a rush. Somehow, not catching her breath or getting the gargantuan body off her, diminished her arm's pain.

The gentle giant rolled off Sally, embarrassed and afraid. "I'm sorry, Ma'am, are you hurt?"

'Am I hurt? I might be dead. I can't breathe; my arms on fire! Hell yes, I'm hurt.' Sally thought this but couldn't say it. Couldn't get her breath back. She thought 1 of 3 things would happen; she would throw up, pass out, or get up and kick this kid in his privates, as hard as she could.

Her breath came back, nausea went away, but her right arm still hurt like hell. The tackle, Kent Whittaker, stayed with Sally. "Don't touch my side, just put your arms under my back and gently, and I mean very gently, lift me into a sitting position." That is accomplished. The pain comes on hard. After a rest, Kent got Sally to her feet. The pain now humming through her body. Sally's knees give out. Kent caught her as she went limp.

Trigby had started attending high school games in the local area. High school sports take on the same importance as university or professional sports in larger towns. It is something to do for Trigby; he doesn't want to wear out his welcome at the Lawsons.

This night he sat in the stands, hands in the pockets of the jacket Mrs. Lawson made him buy. *'What a miserable night.'* At least Trigby has the grandstand's roof; he felt sorry for the players, coaches and cheer squad on the sidelines, standing in the wind and rain. *'What a miserable game, on a miserable night.'* Every time Grays River had the ball, they gave it up. Twice by fumble, once by interception, and once by a blocked punt.

All in the 1st half of the 1st quarter. Naselle's offense wasn't better than Grays River, but at least they held on to the ball. Naselle's defense had done all the scoring.

Trigby stood up to leave; if he stayed through the whole game, he worried the score would be in triple numbers. *'Might as well get coffee and a hot dog on the way out.'* As he got to the aisle, Trigby stopped to watch one last play. Grays River, on their own 20-yard line, right hash mark. Rain coming down hard. "Hut 1, hut 2, hut 3." The quarterback hands off to the fullback, who for, some inexplicable reason, starts running left, straight for the sidelines.

"Wrong way, the wrong way." Trigby finds himself yelling, waving arms above his head. A little embarrassed, he continues down the stairs. Glancing up, he watches the entire Grays River line follow their left guard, halfback and fullback on a suicide attack at their own sidelines. Players crash into other players; players crash into coaches; players crash into cheerleaders.

'What a mess.' Trigby surveys the scene and something clicks. He realizes he is doing a visual triage of a battle scene. Injuries will mostly be minor; bruises and sprains.

There is a woman, not a kid, on the ground by the cheerleaders. Trigby saw her get hit, get hit hard. The player who'd done the damage is trying to get her up. "Hey, hey, don't move her!" The player couldn't hear in the commotion. Trigby leapt over the railing onto the field. Running to the woman. The player got her upright and now she is slipping through his arms, back to the ground.

"Leave her there. Back away, I'll take care of her."

"Yes sir."

"Good, look for this woman's purse. She will want it."

Trigby checked; she is breathing. Her eyes closed; he lifts an eyelid to find a beautiful hazel eye staring back at him.

"Can you talk?"

"Not very well. Can't catch . . . my . . . my breath."

"OK, don't try. You're going to be fine. Let me check a few things."

Trigby starts with her head. No blood, no swelling. "Good."

Next her neck. Same thing, no injury. "Good."

Lower legs and feet, no injuries. He moves his hands over her skirt on both sides. No injuries, no pain reaction, but both her eyes opened. An amazing green, with just a hint of brown.

This part of the examination took a minute. "OK, all good so far. Just 2 more things, arms and torso." From the stands, Trigby had seen her holding her right arm across her chest with her left hand. Even now, she held the arm in the same position. The right arm would be where the injury was. He was sure of this when he first knelt down but wanted to check everything else to know how to proceed.

The left guard, number 76, returned with a brown leather purse. "It's the only one I could find."

"Must be hers. Stick around; I may need you."

In a soft voice, Trigby said, "Ma'am, I'm going to straighten your right arm. Tell me if it hurts."

Trigby gently lifted her right arm off her chest.

Pain shot through Sally. With her left hand, she punched Trigby in the eye.

"HEY, I said tell me, not punch me."

"My arm hurts, bad."

"So does my eye. Number 76, hold her arm."

"I'm not sure I__"

"Do it 76, don't let her hit me again."

"Yes sir."

Trigby took her radial pulse. "Good, no blood vessels impeded. Ma'am, I'm going to check your other arm. 76, hold her fist down." Gently he moved his hand over Sally's forearm.

"OK, Ma'am, what's your name?"

"Sally," she said it slowly, just above a whisper. The pain made her cry.

"OK, Sally, you're coherent with good pulse and color. All of that is good. The problem is your right arm. The bone in your forearm is broken; that's the bad news. The good news, both the ends of the bone at the break are close together. Treatment will probably be an X-ray to make sure it's just 1 break and then a cast. 6 weeks with that and you'll be good as new."

"Thank you."

"I'll need to stabilize the arm and get you to the hospital. 76 bring me a down marker."

Sally, on the turf, Trigby beside her, waiting for the kid to bring the wooden marker.

"OK, break it in half."

Kent, number 76, did it easily. "OK, break in half again. Great. Now, look around the bench; there should be some tape. Hurry, get back soon. Run."

Trigby took off his coat and draped it over Sally.

Kent, back in a flash. Laying the 2 pieces of the marker alongside Sally's forearm, Trigby wrapped it lightly with tape.

"Ok, 76, let's get her up."

"How did you get here, Sally?"

"My truck's in the parking lot."

"Good; when we walk there, 76 and I will help; you hold your injured arm with the other. 76, see that red bike over there; when we get her in the truck, get it and throw it in the bed of the truck. And thanks, you've been a lot of help."

"I'm not sure I can drive." Sally could barely stand.

"I'm sure you can't drive. I'm driving you to the Ilwaco hospital."

"Thank you."

The drive to Ilwaco, mostly silent. Sally thanked Trigby again and again, until he made her stop. "You're welcome. Stop talking, close your eyes and rest." The cab of the truck is its own little universe, windshield wipers slapping back and forth. The glow of the dashboard lights, rain drumming on the cab's roof, heater turned up to high.

"We're here at the hospital, Sally. Don't move; I'll be right back."

Trigby came back with an orderly and a wheelchair. Inside the emergency ward, a doctor and nurse are waiting.

"I'm Doctor Billings; what do we have here."

Trigby replied, "non-displaced fracture of the radial bone. She is coherent, with blood pressure and pulse elevated due to the pain. She'll need something for the pain, an X-ray and cast for the arm."

"Thank you, if you don't mind, I'll check the patient out myself. Please move out to the waiting room."

Trigby sat in the waiting room, which like all ER waiting rooms, has uncomfortable chairs, tattered magazines and a motley group of people waiting. He looks through a month-old Life magazine, next Colliers and finally, Time. Trigby tried reading an article in one of the magazines until he realized he'd read the same page 3 times. He flips the pages, not concentrating. He stopped for a series of Norman Rockwell paintings. So well done! Trigby has always liked them.

After an hour, Dr. Billings came out. "Are you the one that brought a Miss Sally Mathers in?"

"Yes, I'm Trigby Newton; I brought her in."

The 2 men shook hands, "How is she, Doctor?"

"Well, she had elevated blood pressure and pulse. Better now. And a non-displaced fractured radial bone on her right arm. Which is exactly what you told me an hour ago. X-ray shows a surprisingly clean break. I just finished casting the arm. Gave her a solid dose of Demerol for pain."

"Thanks, Doctor."

"Nice work on the splint. If I'm not mistaken, you used a yard marker. Right?"

"All I had to work with."

"Surprised there wasn't something in the locker room."

"Didn't have time to look; she was going into shock."

"And you saved her that. Good on you."

They are now outside, the storm dying down but still breezy. The Doctor took a pack of Lucky Strikes out of his pocket and struggled in the wind to light one. Tried again, failed. Tried again, failed. "Care for a smoke?"

"No thanks, Doctor. I smoke a pipe, left it at home."

"Damn matches. Mr. Newton, it seems you know something about doctoring. Where did you learn?"

"Oregon State and the Army."

"The Army? Medic?"

"Surgeon."

"Well, Dr. Newton, I apologize; you should have__"

"I'm not a doctor now."

"Well hell, you're way too young to ret__"

"Listen Doc; I forgot something in the truck. When can Sally leave?"

"Probably 20 minutes; I want the pain meds to take effect before she's moved."

"Great." Trigby turned and quickly walked away.

The Doctor watched him go; he tried to light his cigarette again and failed. He threw the matches and cigarette in the trash can by the entrance. Went inside, came back out and threw the rest of the pack in the can.

CHAPTER 28

"Turn here."

If not for Sally's direction, Trigby would have missed it. The driveway is hidden by the night and 2 large trees on either side of the drive. A white mailbox just off Highway 4 is the only visible sign of a house.

A fence that needed painting ran the length of the private, graveled drive. Smaller trees marched up the road alongside the fence. Trigby can't see them, but there are fields on either side of the driveway.

200 yards in, the roadway climbed up a small hill to a 2-story farmhouse that also needed painting. A small barn sat alongside the house. Trigby pulled up to the front porch, a single light shining above the door.

"Stay put, Sally; I'll help you out of the truck and up the stairs. I've got your purse."

"Thanks; I feel a little woozy."

Out of the truck and up the stairs to the front door took a while. Sally fumbled with the key until Trigby took it from her and opened the door. Sandy, the golden retriever, scampered wildly to Sally. Then the dog started to growl, deep in her throat.

"Sandy, what are you doing? Stop it this instant."

With that, the dog started barking; she did not like the presence of Trigby. "I'm sorry; she's never like this."

"Women of all ages love me, and most dogs like me, but there have been dissenters in both cases."

"Well, I'm sorry, Mr. . . . I don't even know your name. Let me get my dog under control. Sandy, get over here. Now!" She ordered the dog into the kitchen and shut the door; the dog continued to growl.

"I know your name is Sally Mather, and my name is Trigby Newton."

"Nice to meet you, Mr. Newton and thank you for saving me. I'm not sure I understand what happened. But I know you helped me."

"Glad I could help. Now I should be leaving."

"How will you get home?"

"I'll ride my bike."

"Now? In the dark, Mr. Newton?"

"It's how I got to the game."

"Well, you could sta___, you can take my truck."

"You're too generous; shouldn't let a stranger take your truck."

"If you wanted that old truck, you could have taken it earlier in the evening. Could you give me my purse? Thank you. Here are the keys."

"Thank you, Miss Mather. It will be uncomfortable sleeping tonight; I'd suggest a chair. Is there someone you can call?"

"I have neighbors if I need them."

"OK, I'll be leaving now before your dog tears down the kitchen door."

After several false starts, Sally heard the truck engine catch and pull away.

Saturday morning, 8AM.

Jenny knocks on Trigby's door. "Mom wants to know if you want to come up for breakfast. Bacon and eggs."

"Thanks, tell her I'll be there in 10 minutes."

By the time Trigby gets to the parsonage, Everett Lawson is on his 2nd helping of eggs, bacon and pancakes.

"Thanks for the invitation, Mrs. Lawson."

"Glad you could join us, Trigby. I do have to mention you look a might bit, worse for wear."

"I heard a truck drive up to the church last night and I notice a truck down there now," Everett said between bites.

Jenny sat on the other side of Trigby. "What happened to your eye?"

"A woman hit me in the eye, hard."

"While you were stealing her truck?" Everett again.

"Where is this woman now?" Helen Lawson joined the questioning.

Trigby wondered exactly when the Lawsons had been declared his parents. He sipped his coffee, cut his pancake into squares, had some more coffee and answered.

"Thank you for your interest. To save time, I'll give you the pertinent facts now and you can make up the rest yourselves. At the football game last night, I saved a woman's life after she was mowed down by a gang of testosterone-crazed football players. She had a broken arm, which I stabilized."

"Can you die from a broken arm?"

"Yes, Jenny, you can. And it appears you may grow up to become a prosecuting attorney. As I was saying, after stabilizing the arm, I drove the woman to the Ilwaco hospital."

"Very gallant of you."

"Indeed, Mrs. Lawson. I stayed while they X-rayed the arm and cast it. I drove her home and she offered her truck to me, in appreciation. To answer the question you're about to ask, the woman's name is Sally Masters, no Mathew, no, no, Mather. Sally Mather. Yes, Sally Mather."

"The Mathers just past Grays River?"

"The very one Everett. Whom I will be returning the truck after another pancake, if you left me one."

"I hid a plate for you in the stove."

"Thank you, Jenny. You are a truly, wonderful child."

Trigby turned into Sally Mather's drive; he should have called first. Thought about it but didn't have the phone number. When he got out of the truck, Sally stood at the front door.

"Good morning, Mr. Newton. I heard you come up the drive."

"Good morning to you, Miss Mather."

"Can I offer you a cup of coffee?"

"I'd enjoy that."

"Well, come on in. I've got the dog closed up in the kitchen. Please have a seat; I'll be right back."

But the dog got out of the kitchen. When Sally went in, Sandy came out. Stood 10 feet away from Trigby, with a low growl. Trigby reached in his pocket and pitched a slice of cooked hot dog at the animal. The dog sniffed it, ate it. Trigby pitched another slice, the dog, much closer now, sniffed it, ate it. Trigby placed a slice on the floor next to him. Sandy moved in, ate the slice and sat staring at Trigby.

Sally came out with a coffee pot, went back for cups, went back for cookies. "It's amazing how much harder things are with only 1 working arm. Sandy, how did you get out? Is she bothering you?"

"No, we have reached an agreement." The dog knows she is being talked about; she jumps up on the couch and sidles up to Trigby. "We're best friends now. How is your arm?"

"Well, I'm trying to be a good soldier, but it still hurts. The medicine they gave me makes me goofy."

"Goofy in a pleasant sort of way, Miss Mather. You might try cutting the pills in half but continue taking them; you need to keep in front of the pain."

"Thanks for the advice and your attention. Goodness gracious, Mr. Newton. What happened to your eye?"

"You hit me, hard!"

"I did not."

"Yes, you did. I had to move your broken arm and in reaction to the pain, you used your healthy arm to smack me in the face."

"Wow, I'm so sorry. Can I get you some ice, a steak?"

"The steak maybe later. No ice; I like the way my eye looks. It's the basis of a good story."

"Who have you told this story to?"

"Everybody who asks about my eye."

Sally took Trigby on a tour of the farm. Sandy followed Trigby closely; he'd slip her a hot dog slice on the sly.

"You and Sandy certainly are best friends now."

"Women and dogs of all ages lov__"

"Yes, you told me."

"Thanks for lunch, I should be getting back." Trigby didn't want to leave. The time went by quickly, Sally, wonderful company. "Can I look in on you from time to time?"

"Sure, I would enjoy that. Maybe next weekend. Weekdays are hard for me; when I'm done with the school day, I'm pretty much done for the day."

"How about next Saturday morning?"

"Great. 10 o'clock?"

"Perfect."

"Now that we're making future plans, can we start using 1st names, Sally?"

"Yes, we can, Trigby."

Trigby rassled his bike out of the back of the truck and set off down the drive with Sandy trailing. "Go home now, go home." Sandy finally gave up and headed back.

Columbia River 1942

The sky changed to grey. High clouds, moving in from the Northwest over the Columbia River bar. The day is light, a high over-cast Spring day. Not the dark, close clouds of Winter. The River, mirroring the sky, turned a light grey on top of the waves, green underneath.

Large clouds, puffy and white on the tops, straight and grey on the bottoms. They float over the Willapa Hills across the River from Astoria. Clouds that are more decoration than anything else, harmless, moving with the wind.

Fish and seals own the River. Birds of all kinds, own the sky above. Eagles, hawks, cormorants, seagulls, starlings, ducks and geese in the spring and fall. The eagles fly the highest, patiently circling, waiting, depending on their magnificent eyesight. Their sight is far superior to any other living thing on earth. But gulls are the true flyers, efficient, never tiring, elegant in flight, less so on land. They have truly learned to ride the wind. To use it, not fight it.

The lower Columbia River is emptying out. Tide running to low. Some days the tide runs fast. Those days the 12-foot-high iron channel markers lean over, pushed by the rush of the tide. This morning the River is calm, doing its duty of scouring the estuary in an efficient, composed manner. Pilings that were covered with water earlier this morning are revealed. 10 feet high pilings, shockingly green, covered with algae.

It is the same with sand bars. Dry land emerges from the River during low tide. Many sand bars are long; some run a mile in length, seldom very wide. Some sand bars appear every day, twice a day. Others emerge only on the lowest tides. Many remain hidden under water, sometimes barely covered.

Imagine the amount of water that runs in and out of the Columbia River estuary twice a day. The lower Columbia covers an area 4 to 12 miles wide and at least 20 river-miles in length. The depth runs from a few feet to 42 feet in the shipping channel. Imagine the energy required to move that amount of water.

Tides depend on the moon and rain for swiftness and volume. After a winter storm or a full moon, or worse, both storm and full moon, the River turns angry and fills with debris stolen from the shore. Always grass and bushes, often trees, big trees, torn from the banks, moving fast downstream. Some become caught under piers and bridges.

From small boats, brave entrepreneurs lasso a line around a tree in the River and haul it to shore to be milled into lumber of all dimensions.

Floats, docks and piers also get torn loose by strong tides and head downstream. Along with all manner of trash and debris. All of this; carried by the River. Some of the wreckage travels only a few miles downstream. And some make it to the Pacific and then are beaten back to shore on both sides of the Columbia River's mouth.

But today, the River is calm; light riffles across the wide River.

PART 8

CHAPTER 29

For a man with a very complicated life, Jukka Turpenen is feeling pretty good.

And then things get complicated. Oldest story on earth; man meets woman, and everything changes in his world.

Veiko waited a good while before asking Jukka to dinner. His wife, Helmi, insisted on it; "Veiko, who knows what food that boy gets at the boarding house? Is a wonder you get a day's work from him."

"Helmi, first, he is no boy, grown man. He works hard."

"He works harder with good food. He is sick a lot, from bad food."

"Helmi, a wise man keeps work people and family separate."

"My husband, Veiko, the wise man."

"Helmi, it just th__"

"Veiko, I will expect Jukka for Sunday dinner, 3 o'clock."

"Yes, Helmi."

Jukka walks west from his boarding house on Bond, turns at the *Dough Boy* monument and heads up Alameda Street. Veiko lives in the Union Town neighborhood of Astoria. The name comes from the number of unionized cannery workers who live in the area.

The address Veiko gave him is for a hilltop home up a long flight of steep stairs. '*36 stairs, Veiko must not get old. These steps could kill an old man!*' Jukka prides himself on being in good shape. The stairs brought a bit of humility back to him. The house is bright blue, freshly painted, with a front porch painted white. Jukka carries flowers and a large bottle of beer.

Jukka pauses at the top of the stairs; there is a tiny lawn, freshly mown and then another 8 steps to the porch and front door. Helmi answers the knock.

"Hello, you are Jukka, I am Helmi, Veiko's wife. Come in." Jukka hands Helmi the flowers and wipes his shoes on the outside doormat and the rug inside. He looks up to see Helmi watching him, nodding her head in approval. Veiko sits in his chair, smoking a pipe, his feet on a hassock.

"Veiko, get up and greet our guest and put down that smelly pipe before I throw it out the door."

"Welcome Jukka. You bring Rainer Club beer, thank you, I must be paying you too much."

The inside of the house is uncluttered, almost spartan and amazingly clean. So clean, it makes Jukka uncomfortable. Veiko gives him a tour of the small, tidy home. The front and dining rooms are really 1 room, with a pair of decorative wooden columns on opposing walls acting as a divider. There is a steep set of stairs just inside the front door leading sharply upstairs. *'More stairs,'* Jukka thought, *'these must end in heaven.'* The kitchen is off the dining room and is a testament to Helmi's ability to put out a good meal in a tiny space.

The garden at the back of the house is Veiko's pride and joy. He and Jukka sit in the backyard in straight-back wooden chairs, sharing the bottle of beer in small ceramic mugs. Veiko smokes his pipe. "I can smoke outside, but inside, Helmi gives me trouble."

Jukka noticed the dining table set for 4 people. He wonders who the 4th guest would be. He got his answer when Helmi announced, 'dinner ready.' The grass in the back garden was wet. Veiko takes off his shoes by the back door and Jukka followed suit. As they enter the dining room, seated at the table, a beautiful young woman. Blond hair, dazzling blue eyes, a beauty.

In the time Veiko and Jukka fished together, in true Scandinavian style, Veiko hadn't talked about his home, his wife and certainly not about the blond angel sitting at the table.

"Hello, I'm Dea." She reached out to shake hands with Jukka. He couldn't seem to find his voice. "And you are?"

After an uncomfortable pause, "I am Jukka." His own voice sounded odd.

Once Helmi served the food and Jukka found his voice, the dinner went on pleasantly. Dea, a 1st generation American girl, obviously from Scandinavian roots. She has her own mind, is well-read on many subjects and appears unaware of her beauty. Her name had been a source of tension between her parents. Veiko wanted a traditional name; Helmi wouldn't stand for it.

"Veiko, you give this baby old world name and she will spend her life spelling it out. Our baby will be American girl, American woman. Do not argue with me on this."

"Yes, Helmi."

And so, it begins. Jukka is invited to dinner every other Sunday; now he brings flowers for both Helmi and Dea. And he helps Dea wash and dry the dinner dishes. They spend time together in the garden; talking, laughing, getting to know one another.

"Veiko, may I take Dea to the movies on Saturday?"

"Let us be about fishing, not about my daughter. But yes, I think you may; I will have to ask Helmi."

Helmi reluctantly agreed.

Jukka walked to Union Town and up the formidable stairs that led to Dea's house. Veiko answered the knock and led Jukka to the front room, offering him a shot glass of Aquavit. "They call this a 'hard hook' in the old country, Jukka."

The 2 men waited patiently for Dea to come down. Helmi instructed her daughter; "make the young man wait. Do not rush to the door."

Jukka chatted with Helmi and Veiko out of politeness; when Dea couldn't stand it any longer, she came down the stairs. Lovely, dressed in a bright blue dress, Dea looked like the grown-up version of the child Veiko and Helmi had raised. She made Veiko proud, Helmi worried.

Jukka and Dea left the house and made their way down the steep stairs. Going down the stairs, remarkably as tiring as going up. They took the streetcar over Bond Street to downtown. They both enjoyed watching Yankee Doodle Dandy, at the Egyptian-themed Liberty Theater. Jukka sprung for Coca-Cola and popcorn at intermission.

After a shared sundae at Lawson's, the streetcar took them back to Union Town.

At the front door, neither knew what to do. Both knew something should be done but couldn't decide what. In the end, Dea put out her hand and Jukka took it in one hand and patted it with his other.

"Thank you for taking me to the movies. I had a very nice time, Jukka."

"Thank you for coming with me."

"Good night."

"Good night."

Dea waited until Jukka walked down the stairs; he looked back and waved. She opened the door, took off her coat and hung it on the coat rack. Only the light from the kitchen is on. Dea walked toward it.

"You are home."

Dea gasped. She turned quickly and turned on the light. Her parents sat in the front room; they had been sitting in the dark, waiting for her to come home.

"Did you have a nice time?" Veiko asked.

"Yes, Father, I did."

"Was Jukka a gentleman?" Helmi asked.

"Yes, Ma'am."

Veiko said, "good, I will not have to push him overboard tomorrow."

With his interest in Dea growing by leaps and bounds, Jukka has less time to concentrate on his mission. There aren't enough hours in Jukka's day between Dea, fishing and reconnaissance for his country. He made up a story about a cousin who had immigrated to Aberdeen, Washington. The lie made the monthly trip to report to his superiors easier to sell. He wished he had thought of it before.

CHAPTER 30

Another month roared by. Another trip to Aberdeen for Jukka. Another drilling from the man with the slate-grey eyes. The plan is ready to move into action. Every part of the attack thought out, looking for any problem that could occur. Everything re-examined, and then re-examined again. Jukka grilled on all aspects, those he was responsible for and those he was not.

Jukka's desire for Dea is at fever pitch. If a hundred things were different, Dea and Jukka could move forward to a life together. But not with a war on. Not with all of the lies Jukka had told everyone.

On the bus ride back to Astoria, Jukka and his life became unglued. The war isn't stopping for him; it's starting for him. The dream he's been living, a joke. To think he could set aside the blood and soil of the Fatherland and slip into a new American life, is childish thinking.

'I am an SS officer, sworn to Fuhrer and Country. Not possible to just slip away from those responsibilities. I've

lied to everyone so often; I started to believe the lies myself. And now truth slaps me in the face.'

The woman next to Jukka on the bus could tell something was bothering the young man. Bothering him deeply. She got up and moved 4 rows back. She had her own problems.

Back to Jukka:

'I could slip away, run away from everything. How could I? Where would I go? They'd find me and kill me. If they couldn't find me, they'd imprison my family in Germany. Kill them. I could not run with Dea. Leave her; better that way. I could come back to her after the damn war ends. Come back to what? Would she want me back after I left without a word? No, she would not.

Every new thought brought more problems, more guilt, more anguish. Thousands of thoughts, one after another. Ideas piling on top of each other, each contradicting another. *I'm losing my mind.'*

The bus roared through the tunnel past Chinook, Washington, heading for the ferry landing in Megler, Washington. Astoria came in to view across the River. It is a different view in wartime. Black-out curtains in all homes, no streetlights, Astoria is a adrift on a dark peninsula.

On the outside deck of the ferry, Jukka felt the wind on his face, smelled the tang of salt and river water mixing in the River. It calmed him. He managed to get his options in order. No way to be reassigned. Jukka could feel the slate grey eyes from the meeting, burning into his mind. Jukka's reassignment would be a bullet in his head; his body dumped in the River.

That left honoring his oath and fulfilling his new mission. At the same time remaining true to his love for Dea and his feelings for her family. Hoping and praying this would somehow work out. Hope and prayer against common sense.

Veiko finally bought a 4-year-old Chevrolet from Lovell Auto. He'd wanted a sedan for years, tired of driving the truck everywhere. Tired of Helmi's complaining about riding in the truck everywhere.

It is a surprise for his wife, Helmi. She is surprised and not happy.

"How can we afford this luxury? We have the pickup."

"The pickup you have complained about for 7-years? That pickup?" Veiko is right; Helmi hates the pickup, embarrassed to be seen in it. She makes Veiko park the truck 3 blocks away from the Church every Sunday.

"OK, Mr. Big Spender, we live in the new car. Sell the house."

The discussion went on for a good 30 minutes in Finnish. The language for serious discussions. Or when either Veiko or Helmi got mad.

Veiko parked the new Chevrolet at the bottom of his stairs and put a tarp over it at night. Veiko loved his new car. He washed it every Sunday afternoon and drove to the docks to show it off to his friends. Helmi and Veiko got to Church early so the Chevrolet could be parked close. "Why not drive the automobile into the Church, Veiko? Park in front of the altar."

Veiko still took the pickup to the dock on fishing days. One day he found another pickup truck parked next to his spot. The 1938 Willys-Overland looked worn but clean, recently washed.

"Jukka, who's truck?"

"Mine, Sir."

"Yours, Jukka? Now I know I pay you too much."

"My cousin in Aberdeen, sold to me cheap. I pay him bit by bit."

"That is a good cousin."

Now with his own transportation, Jukka takes Dea on a 'Sunday Drive' every week. They drive the Oregon beaches between Gearhart and Fort Stevens, stopping for a picnic at the wreck of the Peter Iredale. They also drive on THE WORLDS LONGEST BEACH (or so they say), the 26-mile beach on the Long Beach Peninsula in Washington.

Dea loves Seaside in Oregon and Long Beach in Washington, both tourist beach towns. Cotton candy, bumper cars, Ferris wheels, candy shops, dozens of places to eat – good, bad and indifferent. And, of course, beaches. Dea loves it all. But the town they visit the most is Naselle, Washington.

"What a surprise, Jukka; here we are in Naselle. Again. On Parpilla Road. Again."

"I like Naselle, Dea."

"Too much. Do you want to move to Naselle? Buy a house on Parpilla Road? Move away from me?"

"Questions, questions. Because you ask, I want to move to Naselle, live on Parpilla Road and marry you." And there it is, out in the open.

"Jukka, Jukka. I'm not . . . I might go to coll__ you must talk to Dad."

"I want to talk to you first, then Veiko. But I surprise you; please think it over."

Things became uncomfortable between Jukka and Dea. Jukka didn't dare bring up marriage again and Dea needed time to herself.

"Jukka, have not seen you around the house lately."

"I've been busy, Veiko."

"Busy or in trouble?"

"Ask your daughter."

Veiko did not ask his daughter; he asked his wife. She replied, "Veiko, if you pay more attention to daughter and wife, instead of new car and fishing, you will know what happens."

"I pay attention now, Helmi."

"Jukka asked your daughter for marriage."

"He should talk to me first."

"Yes, he should have asked your permission. What would your answer be?"

"I think it would be a good marriage; I would say yes."

"Dea is a child, Veiko. I say no."

"What does Dea say?"

Dea hasn't said anything. She has a plan for herself and marriage now isn't part of it. Dea feels honored by the asking but uncertain of her commitment. And now her parents are involved. Helmi against it, and Dea knowing Veiko, is sure he'd be for it.

Many of her friends were amazed Dea didn't jump at the chance to marry Jukka.

'Strong, good looking, with a job!'

'He's a man, Dea, not like the boys in our class.'

'Golly, can I call him?'

But Dea's best friend agreed with her choice. "He's the 1st real boyfriend you've had. There will be more. Wait, follow your plan, not his."

Dea hasn't given up on Jukka. The marriage proposal so out of the blue, it confused her, shook her up. She didn't want to lose Jukka, but Dea wanted a boyfriend, not a husband.

'I ask a woman to marry, and she gets mad at me!' Dea's reaction is something Jukka cannot understand. *'I risk everything for her, and now what? What should I do?'*

"Jukka, we take on fuel on the starboard, not port." Jukka is getting a bit sloppy on the boat and it irks Veiko. "Think Jukka; we are fishing now. Private life is later."

Helmi didn't care who has hurt feelings, who is irked; she didn't care. Anything that could put a halt to this budding romance, fine with her.

There was an attempt at a Sunday dinner; it didn't turn out well. Awkward at best.

Helmi made her famous 'Finnish Chicken.' Jukka and Veiko had shots of Aquavit on the back porch. The sparse conversation, all about fishing.

After what seemed like a century, Dea came downstairs. Jukka remembered the 1st time, such a short time ago, he'd seen her come down these same stairs.

"Hello, Jukka."

"Hello, Dea."

Long silence.

Dea tried her best to keep the conversation going, Veiko helped her as much as he could. Helmi glared at Jukka. By turns, Jukka seemed mad, sad, bewildered.

"Veiko, help me with the dishes."

"I don't do__"

"Now, Veiko."

"Yes, Helmi."

With her parents gone to the kitchen, Dea leaned closer to Jukka.

"I'm sorry, I need time Jukka. I like you, enjoy our time together, but that's all I can give you now. Marriage is . . . . is"

"I should not have asked. Too soon for you."

"We can still see each other. Spend some time together."

"Can we go for a Sunday drive today?"

"I'm sorry, Jukka, not today."

And not the next Sunday or the Sunday after that.

I want to marry you.' Those 5 words tore the romance apart. No more Sunday dinners or drives; they saw each other from time to time downtown. One time they had a Coca-Cola at Woolworths. Dea started to see a boy from her class; he is going to the University of Oregon in the fall.

Jukka takes solace in work. He works harder for Veiko (while looking for jobs on other boats) and works hard for his master's in Aberdeen.

"You look at the charts more than I do, Jukka. Are you searching for buried treasure?"

"I want to know the River, like you do, Veiko."

With romance out of the way, Veiko is pleased with the work and interest Jukka is showing on the boat.

Jukka is sick of it all. Everything. And most of all, himself.

CHAPTER 31

Axle Bjork is a friend of Veiko's. Axle is a house painter. They both belong to the Scandinavian Benevolent Society, which is the oldest lodge in Astoria. Veiko hired Axle to paint his house. Axle thought he didn't charge Veiko enough, Veiko thought Axle charged too much. It strained the relationship.

"I'd only do this price for an SBS member, Veiko; I make nothing on this deal."

"Thank you, Axle. I hate to think how much you'd charge someone not in the SBS. I want you to paint my house, not every house in the neighborhood."

Axle heard there were engine problems on Veiko's boat and the problems kept him and his boat at the dock. Axle felt he should stop by, for Veiko's morale, if nothing else.

"Hello, Axle."

"Hello, Veiko. Did you buy a new car with the money you saved having me paint the house?"

"No, I paid you 3 times what I should have because I feel sorry for you. And what did my good deed get me? I'll tell you, my engine is no-go. And I have no money to fix it."

Jukka, hunched over in the engine compartment and covered in oil and sweat, heard all of this. *'These 2 are friends? Might be friendlier as enemies.'*

"Jukka, come and join my friend for coffee."

"If it's all the same to you, Veiko, I'll keep working on the motor so we can go out and catch fish, make money."

"OK, Jukka."

In a soft voice, Veiko said to Axle, "my mate has a good head on his shoulders."

"Or he's tasted your coffee," Axle replied.

After 2 cups of coffee and 30 minutes of wrangling back and forth, Axle said goodbye to his friend and decided to head for home. He walked East along the River waterfront towards the ferry landing at the foot of 14th Street.

On the walk, Axle, passes a row of canneries; noisy and smelly. Veiko had told him, "Hell yes; they smell; it smells like money." Unlike earlier canneries, these are modern, mechanical, motorized. And incredibly busy. 3 shifts a day, never stopping, always pushing.

Axle lives in Chinook, across the River from Astoria. He is a methodical painter; exact, painstaking and slow. All the hustle and bustle in Astoria makes him feel tired. The weather today, foggy and wet, not suited for house painting. He left his truck on the Washington side of the River. The fare is cheaper if you walk on. He enjoyed the ferry ride across the River and now he's ready to get back on the ferry and head home.

There's a 20-minute wait for the ferry. Axle gets out his cigarette papers and tobacco pouch. It takes a couple of matches to get the cigarette going. Looking up, he sees someone he knows.

'Miller, you lying son-of-a-bitch, where is my 20 bucks!"

"Shit, Axle, that's one hell of a way to say hello to a friend. And stop shouting."

"I wouldn't be shouting if you were a friend. Where is my $20?"

"I paid you back . . . didn't I?"

"Hell, no you didn't pay me back. Stupid of me to lend it to you in the first place."

"OK, OK, Axle, I owe you $20__"

"You've owed it for months__"

"OK, you're right but I don't have it now. Can we trade?"

"Trade for what?"

"I got a job at Stevenson's cannery. Night shift. Come by tomorrow night, quarter to 12. Just before the shift change. I'll get you some fish."

"How many and what kinda fish?"

"Axle, you drive a hard bargain; 2 salmon, big ones."

"Make it 4 salmon and some sturgeon. And I don't drive a hard bargain, I lent you $20, and instead of getting $20 back, I'm an accessory to robbery."

"You what?" Doris, Axle's wife.

"I have to go to Stevenson cannery in Astoria at 11:45 tomorrow night to get some fish. Doris, it's in payment for the $20 I lent Miller."

"I believe you get dumber every year, and here is the proof. Who is dumber, you loaning money to a no-good scoundrel or the scoundrel who repays you with stolen fish? Dumb and dumber!"

Axle has a problem; Doris is right. The other concern is timing. The last ferry out of Astoria is at 12:30PM. He must get the fish from the cannery and return to the ferry landing by 12:20 at the latest. Shouldn't be a problem.

But it becomes a problem, a huge problem. Axle stands where Miller told him, underneath a 2nd story sliding door at the cannery. The night is dark and windy; thank goodness no rain. He hears the big sliding wood door open and then a strange rushing sound. The sound a frozen salmon makes when dropped from a 2nd story. It barely missed Axle's head. *'Is he trying to kill me, to not pay me back?'*

That thought interrupted by another frozen salmon falling on his shoulder. The pain raced down his shoulder, arm and fingers. Next, 2 more salmon come raining down and 2 small sturgeon. Axle danced around and managed not to get hit again. The overhead door closed.

Yes, he got more than $20 worth of fish, but now what? Axle has to get all of it to the ferry in a hurry. First, he rolled the sturgeon in his jacket, then hid the salmon under a parked car and prayed the car wouldn't be moved.

Axle picked up the sturgeon, holding them precariously with both hands and ran like a linebacker with an intercepted pass for the ferry. He left the sturgeon behind a trash can at the ferry dock.

At 55, Axle hasn't done much running lately. The runback for the salmon took a lot out of him.

He took his shirt off and rolled the salmon up. Bare-chested, he made the return trip to the ferry dock, exhausted. Time, 12:26. Running up the 'Walk On Ramp,' he threw the salmon onboard. Raced back down the ramp and snatched up the sturgeon. Time 12:28. Axle summoned the last bit of resolve and headed up the ramp. His resolve isn't that of an All-American half-back; it is the resolve of a 55-year-old smoker, drinker, whose idea of exercise is walking the dog. Axle, nose running, coughing between pants, stumbling, almost falling, trying to run up the ramp. Time, 12:29. The auto deck closed, lines cleared, whistle blowing, and the ferry is about to leave the dock.

"Damn it, do not shut that gate." The deck hand looked up. Axle leapt into the man and the fish spilled on the ferry's deck.

Axle sat bare-chested on the outside deck, freezing, for the 40-minute ride to the Washington shore. A couple of people walked by and stared. Axle said, "I got myself salmon and sturgeon."

PART 9

CHAPTER 32

The Game Warden for Wahkiakum County is Bill Young. Tall, broad-shouldered, with a certain look that indicates he'd just as soon fight as talk to you. A man of indeterminate age, north of 50 is about as close as you'll get. Middle-aged, but with a rock-hard body. Odd physique for a man who spends 8 hours a day behind a desk or driving the county's back roads. His muscles come from his hobby, chopping firewood. Every morning, for an hour, chopping and stacking wood. Every evening, for an hour, more chopping, more stacking.

Interesting that Bill's house doesn't have a fireplace or wood stove. His wife doesn't like wood for cooking or heating. Too dirty, smokey and a half-dozen other reasons. She had the fireplace in the living room bricked shut. Replaced it with oil heat and a GE stove.

Bill gives away almost all the wood he chops. If he doesn't like you, he'll still chop the wood but make you pay for it.

Game Warden Bill Young pulled over the jacked-up pickup on a dusty logging road. The truck has 2 long rifles in the back window, a driver and 1 passenger. Hunting season over months ago.

"Hi, boys." Bill can smell whiskey, sees the Jim Beam bottle peeking out from under the truck seat.

"What you want?"

Bill moves upwind from the driver. "Just wanted to have a little chat with you 2."

"Well, I ain't in a talking mood and get the hell off my running board."

"My feet are on the ground."

The interaction went much easier after this exchange.

Everett Lawson, the minister, Arnold Butler, the local vet and Sam Jackson, Wahkiakum County sheriff, have a monthly breakfast. They'd started this tradition a decade ago when they'd worked on a school bond drive that failed.

When Arnold arrived, Everett and Sam had already ordered; coffee, bacon, sausage, pancakes and hash browns. Arnold ordered water, dry toast and a poached egg.

Sam and Everett seem to be in the middle of a long discussion.

"Hell, Ev, I'm not afraid of dying. Just worried my wife will sell my guns for what I told her I paid for them."

"Clear reason for concern, Sam."

Arnold felt the need to move the conversation. "I heard Bill Young is quitting as Game Warden."

Sam's response, "about time."

"How old is Bill?" Arnold asking.

"Older than dirt," Sam again.

"Well, the state will need somebody to replace him. Any ideas?" Arnold is the practical one of the bunch.

"It won't be an easy job and doesn't pay much. People up in the hills just as soon shoot the Game Warden as out-of-season deer. Best part of the job is the free pickup and free, non-rationed gas."

"Good points, Sam, but no potential candidate. Everett, how about you?"

"Me, let's see. Sam, pass me the syrup, please. Not much pay, free truck and gas. I've got the same job, except for the free truck and gas."

"Heck, Ev, if you think your fit enough to tramp through the wilderness in all kinds of bad weather, chasing some wily, armed bastard . . . sign up."

"Thank you, Sam. It's not that I couldn't perform well at that job, but I have a flock to attend to. I do have an excellent candidate, however, Trigby Newton."

"Excellent, Everett. I wanted to suggest him initially, but I enjoy your colorful banter. I'll call Fish & Game in the morning."

"Ev, Arnold, I got just 1 question. Who the hell is Trigby Newton, and where did that name come from?"

"Sam, we will tell you all about Trigby, right Everett?"

And they did tell Sam a lot about Trigby Newton. A lot, but not all of it.

And that's how Trigby Newton became the Game Warden for Wahkiakum County. His training consisted of a few days driving around dirt and gravel backroads with his predecessor, Bill Young.

"Here's the way it is, Trigby; 90% of the people you'll meet in the field will like you and appreciate what you're doing. The other 10% are criminals or clueless; either way, poachers and they won't like you, might even hate you."

"OK," Trigby wonders where this training session is going.

Bill drove with his left hand on the steering wheel and his right, holding a coffee cup; washed once during the Coolidge administration. "Poachers are a big group of people. Some don't know when a season starts or stops, and some don't care. Others are fishing in season and catch a fish that is out of season. Say they catch an out-of-season 60-pound chinook salmon. No way they're gonna throw that back. Never catch a salmon that big again. So, they keep it and I arrest them for poaching."

Trigby thought he should say something just to keep up his side of the conversation but Bill is off again.

"Fish or game always look the biggest out of season. And you gotta look for the dumb shits that net a stream, in or out of season. The other reason people poach is to feed a family. I feel for them. Give them a break or 2. Or tell them to hunt over in Pacific County."

"Will tha__"

"The damndest thing that just started is cedar theft. Felling cedar trees off property that ain't theirs. Always cutting these trees after midnight, you catch them by the bright lights they use. Gotta be bright, so they don't cut off somebody's hand or lose the tree they just cut."

"Any time you give a ticket or make an arrest, Trigby, be sure you're in control of the situation. Know how many there are and where they're at. Make sure your weapons are loaded. Don't aim your weapon unless you're going to shoot. It's 1 thing to shoot a man on purpose and another to shoot a man by accident. By accident, causes a bunch of paperwork."

"Bill, this Jeep rides a little rough."

"Didn't take you for a city boy, Trigby. This job is walking, riding or sitting; if any of that is hard on your butt, get a pillow."

"Thanks for the heartfelt advice, Bill. I was thinking of shocks for the Jeep."

"I was thinking the same thing, 3 years ago. Put in a requisition, haven't heard back."

The last joint tour Bill Young and Trigby took was a night-time raid. Reports of out-of-season elk hunters past Palermo Mountain, in the valley by Dell Creek. Bill and Trigby set out at sunset, the Jeep loaded with sandwiches, coffee, shotguns, pistols and ammunition. Bill, as always, drove and seemed to be on a mission. Tonight, not much chit-chat. "Trigby, I know where these bastards are."

On the roughest road yet, which said a lot, the Jeep took them to the top of a high ridge. Looking down into a narrow valley, a campfire at a distance could be seen. Along with a Ford pickup of indefinite age and 2 pup tents.

"I told you they were dumb shits! Campfire at night; it's like they want to get caught."

"Bill, what's the plan?"

"The plan is to drive down into that valley with the Jeep's lights out. You're going to walk ahead of me, holding a flashlight, pointing not up or out but straight down at your feet. We're crossing a couple of streams and a fair size river on the way down; I'll be in the Jeep, you'll be wet."

An hour later, they are at the bottom. Each water crossing took a great deal of time and deliberation to get across. Bill remained dry in the Jeep, Trigby wet. Bill is right; this group of 3 poachers didn't care much for security. Trigby uses his binoculars to watch the camp from 3 different vantage points. Nobody on guard, the only time a poacher gets up is to grab the bottle of booze that another poacher is reluctant to share.

Bill, in a whisper, "Trigby, it's your job now. I'll slither around the back of the camp. Now you keep control of the situation. Speak with authority. If things go haywire and I have to shoot, drop-down flat; that way I won't hit you and vice/versa. If it comes to shooting, remember this isn't a Western movie. Nothing fancy; aim center of the body and keep firing."

"Yes, sir." *'Good God Almighty, how did I get into this?'*

Trigby moved into the camp; slowly, carefully.

"Howdy boys, I'm the Game Warden and I'm here to arrest you."

3 men resting on bedrolls, rifles beside them, good campfire going.

"What the hell did you say?"

"I said you have 2 elk heads, 5-points on each, out of season. No meat in sight. Trophy poaching, that's the worst crime there is in my book. Now we're about to find out who the dumbest person is. That's the person who doesn't follow my orders and that's the person I shoot in the balls."

"Who says you're gonna shoot anybody? It's 3 against 1 and our damn rifles are sitting next to us."

Trigby's shotgun is open, laying over his left arm. He raises the arm in a swift, efficient action that locks the gun into place. With his thumb, Trigby cocked both barrels. The sound seemed to fill the night.

"Good point, well-spoken. I considered that; I've got a side-by-side double barrel LC Smith shotgun loaded with 00 buckshot. Now, most likely, I could hit 2 of you with the left barrel and certainly blow the head off the 3rd with the right barrel. We will see, or you can sit up, put hands behind your heads, fingers laced."

And that's when a loud growl came from behind the men, followed by a ratty-looking German Shepherd, ready to attack.

"What you gonna do now, Mr. Game Warden?"

Trigby got a smoked hot dog slice out of his right pocket and tossed it to the dog. The dog caught it in the air. Trigby threw another; the dog caught it.

"I've made a new friend. What are you going to do?"

2 of the men had their hands behind their heads; the 3rd, who had spoken up, slowly did the same.

Bill came out of the bushes behind the camp. "Could have used your help, Bill."

"You didn't need it, far as I could see. Nice job."

"Well, keep your rifle on these idiots while I handcuff them."

"Before you do Trigby, I need to address them. I will not have the bed of my pristine vehicle defiled by your stinking garments. Remove shirts, pants and boots. Now!"

The Jeep is washed and brushed out every year or so, whether it needs it or not.

"The other thing I want you dumb shits to think about is that in addition to the fine and jail time you got coming, you got the forfeiture of your Ford pickup. If it's stolen, hell, we won't see you in this county for a decade."

The 2-truck caravan headed out after the camp tidied up, fire put out. Trigby drove the Jeep, with 3 nearly naked poachers and 2 bloody elk heads in the back. The German Shepard rode in the cab with Trigby.

Bill Young rode in the much newer Ford. He kept the headlights on high beam, washing the poachers in startingly white light. It is comforting for Bill to know he is passing on his life-long career to someone who cares as much about it, as he does.

CHAPTER 33

For the 1st time in a long time, Trigby's life has a pattern. Up at 6:30, coffee and breakfast with the 7AM crowd at Mandy's Cafe. Each morning hour seems to have a different group of men at the café.

By 8, if Trigby isn't in the field, he is behind his desk in the small office in the basement of Wahkiakum County Courthouse. He looks to have paperwork done by 10, the appointed time for his morning coffee break at the same café. This is a different group than at the 7AM gathering.

Sam Jacobs, the Sheriff, presides over the diverse 10AM group; it includes Trigby, Lenard Larsen, the head of the volunteer fire department and Arnold Butler, the county veterinarian. Arnold is there mostly to keep things moving in an orderly fashion. Every now and again, a county commissioner will attend. Trigby has been bringing along the German Shepard he'd rescued from the poachers. It is part of Trigby's socialization program. Once he's trained the dog to his satisfaction, Trig plans to give the dog to Jenny, if her parents agree.

"Are you bringing that damn dog in here again, Trigby? We DO NOT allow dogs."

"Well hell, Mandy, you let Lenard and me in."

"Good point, Trigby. You, Lenard and the damn dog, get out." Mandy said this with a smile and a wink. She brings 4 coffees and a small bowl of scraps for the dog.

"What's the name of this animal that is basically skin and bones?"

"I call him Teddy." Jenny had given the dog the name after she learned Trigby's middle name, Theodore.

"Let me look at him," Arnold, the vet said. "Come here, Teddy."

"Hey, Arnie, will you bill me for this?"

"Yes, Trigby, I'll bill you and hopefully, you will pay me. Are you feeding him on the diet I gave you?"

"Yes."

"Giving plenty of water?"

"No, all he'll drink is wine."

"If the dog's examination is over, I got something for Trigby."

"Tell me, Sheriff."

"The folks way up on Grays River Road are shooting at dusk."

"As big a group of inbred miscreants as you'll ever want to meet."

"Thank you, Lenard. As I was saying, they shoot simultaneously to make it hard to tell where the shots are coming from. Since they're shooting at game, it's up to you to put a stop to it, Trigby."

"Thank you, Sheriff; exactly how am I to do this?"

"You're a smart boy, Trigby. You'll figure it out."

"Remember, Jenny, you're in charge. Speak with authority."

"Teddy, come." The dog ambled up to Jenny and she latched a lead on his collar.

"Teddy, heel." Jenny and Teddy marched around the front yard.

"Now, make him sit." And the dog did. They went through the commands and finally, Teddy got his hot dog treat, followed by a rousing game of fetch. Teddy, Jenny and Trigby tried to get in a 20-minute workout every day.

Everett and Helen Lawson watched their young daughter drill the large dog.

"I'm afraid of that dog and Jenny."

"It looks to me like the dog is afraid of Jenny. At the least, very respectful."

Teddy had been sleeping in Trigby's room in the basement of the church.

"I just know he's going to give the dog to Jenny."

"Oh, I don't think so, dear."

"Well, Jenny, you've learned a lot and Teddy responds to you. He knows you're the boss. If you think you can handle the responsibility of a dog, I'd be all for it. Let's go ask your parents."

"I knew it, that darn dog and you, Trigby, I knew it," Helen sighed.

Trigby, Jenny and Teddy stand at attention at the Lawson's back door. The 3 are a pitiful sight. Trigby looking at his feet, Jenny starting to tear up and the dog staring at Helen, right into her soul.

Helen knows the outcome but wants to get as many conditions as possible before she relents. "The dog stays out of the house. Jennifer is responsible completely for the walking, feeding and bathing of the dog. And poop patrol."

"I will Mom, I promise." Jenny broke out into a huge smile.

Teddy walks over to Helen and lays down at her feet, tail wagging.

Trigby stopped by the school during afternoon recess. Sally is in her classroom sipping tea and grading papers.

She has gotten used to the German Shepard accompanying Trigby.

"Where's your dog?"

"Not my dog. I gave it to my friend, Jenny."

'Ah, the mysterious, Jenny.' Sally has heard the name before.

"I thought you loved that dog."

"I do. Jenny's good with him. The dog's name is Teddy."

"You mention Jenny a lot, Trig. Any chance I could meet her."

"Sure."

"When?"

"She gets out of school in an hour."

"She teaches?"

"Probably could. I'll be back in an hour to pick you up."

Trigby picked up Sally an hour and a half later. "Took me that long to wash and clean out the Fish & Game truck, sorry." On the short drive to the Lawsons, they talked about their day. Sally, about her class, Trigby, about his gallant efforts to enforce the laws regarding fish and game.

Trigby pulled into the small parking area between the Church and the Lawson's parsonage. "Trig, you live here? It's a nice house."

"I live in the basement of the Church."

A child opened the front door of the house and skipped down the walkway to Sally and Trigby. "Hi, Trigby."

"Hi yourself. Jenny, meet my friend, Sally."

'The famous Jenny.' Sally is more than a little embarrassed.

"Sally, meet my friend Jenny." The 2 shook hands.

"Meet my dog. Teddy, come."

The large dog leapt off the porch and made a kamikaze run at the small group. Sally braced herself for impact. "Teddy, sit," said Jenny in a stern voice. The dog came to an instant stop.

By this time, the Lawsons had joined the group and are introduced.

"Miss Mather, we have heard so much about you. If Trigby had given us some warning, I could have made something for us."

"Don't worry about me, Mrs. Lawson. I'm used to Trigby's last-minute ideas."

"Let's go inside, I have a couple of slices of apple pie and we can get away from that darn dog."

"My Mom thinks 'darn dog' is Teddy's name. It's Teddy." Jenny said this to Sally with a serious tone in her voice.

"Jenny, sometimes I think of Trigby as that darn man."

"Amen, sister. Let's go inside," this from Helen Lawson. The 2 women went inside and over pie and coffee; Sally Mather learned a lot about Trigby Newton.

"Sally's pretty, Trigby."

"I know, Jenny."

And another part of Trigby's new life started.

Sally invited the Lawsons over for dinner on Friday night. The next week, Helen Lawson invited Sally and Trigby to Sunday dinner. The week after that, Jenny had a birthday party. Sally Mather, the guest of honor.

As a gift, Sally gave the birthday girl the bike she rode at the same age. "I've been saving it all these years for someone. And that is you, Jenny."

"Thank you, Miss Mather, but I don't know how to ride a bike. Mom says it's too dangerous."

"I talked to your mother and she said if I taught you, she would be OK with you owning a bike."

"You're the best, Miss Mather!"

"Be sure and tell Trigby that."

CHAPTER 34

"Who goes out on a night like this?"

"Brave people, who appreciate good music."

It is an unusual October night; thunder, lightning, pounding rain. The rain, normal; thunder and lightning unusual.

"Sally, maybe they'll be back on a better night."

"Trig, if you're afraid of the weather, I can drive, or you can stay home hiding under the covers."

"I'll have you know, I've survived hurricanes and cyclones an__"

"Aren't they the same?"

"OK, OK, I'll drive."

Trigby driving, rain pounding down. Every time he slows down, the wipers slow down; when he speeds up, the wipers run faster. To be able to see, Trigby drives faster than he wants. His fingers have a death grip on the steering wheel.

"So, tell me, who are we risking life and limb to see?"

"Dave Martin and the Fabulous 5."

"Who the heck is Dave Martin, Sally?"

"A blues shouter and red-hot guitar player from Compton, California."

"And the Fabulous 5?"

"The backing band, 5 women."

"Sounds interesting."

"Glad you're showing interest, Trigby, must be the women. I like Dave, I've been following him for years. He comes to Long Beach, Longview and Portland in the spring and fall. Every couple of years, he has a new band."

"You follow this, Dave Martin?"

"I usually see him in Long Beach and the next day in Longview."

"Sally, you say you like Dave, in a romantic way?"

"No, jealous boy, in a musical way. He's not my type."

"Exactly what is your type?"

"Smart, strong and rich. And afraid of inclement weather."

Dave Martin appears at the Elks Club in Long Beach, Washington. Inside, a small foyer packed with people. The meeting hall is through a double door; the bar is to the left. A stage 4 feet high, at the far end. The dance floor is in front of the stage. Small tables run down either side of the hall, with a cluster of tables by the bar.

Making their way through the foyer, everyone seems to know Sally.

"Hey, Sally!"

"I knew you'd be here, Sally."

"Good to see you, Ingrid. Harry, not so good to see you, but what can I do?"

"What can you do? Give me a big hug and a kiss on the cheek. If you kiss me on the lips, we'd run away and you'd have a life full of misery."

"Your wife, standing next to you there, Harry, has told me all about the misery and she still loves you. How are you, Ingrid?"

"I'm fine; who is this handsome man you're sporting?"

"He's on probation. I'll introduce you after I get my table situated."

She directs Trigby through the double doors to a table at the edge of the dance floor, against the wall. Stenciled black letters on the tabletop read: IF YOU ARE SEATED HERE AND YOUR NAME ISN'T SALLY MATHER, YOU ARE AT THE WRONG TABLE.

"Sally, you're a bit of a regular here, aren't you?" Trigby asked.

"Damn right, and proud of it."

Sally left her hat, gloves and jacket on the table. Trigby did the same.

"There are 4 chairs here; who sits in the other chairs?"

"Men waiting to dance with me."

"Howdy folks, I'm Dave Martin, and I'm the luckiest man in the world! Let me introduce the 5 fabulous women in the band!"

1 by 1, the Fabulous 5 come onstage. 1st, the violin player, standing "5 feet, nothing," according to Dave. "She's petite, she's a helluva poker player, and plays the daylights out of that violin." Dave isn't exaggerating; she can make that violin do everything but talk, leaning

forward as if playing into a strong headwind. 6 months later, she will be dead by suicide.

Next, the bass player, Bernice, is introduced and then the 2nd guitar. Dave says, "Betsy, she's always pushing me; I don't mind, I encourage her," Finally, Dave introduces the drummer, Dixie.

Dixie; tall, trim, beautiful pale face, highlighted with dark red lipstick, long black hair, secured with a red pick. She is dressed in a black western suit, with red trim and snaps. Red cowboy boots finish off the outstanding outfit. Every pair of male eyes in the audience follow her across the stage to get seated behind her drum kit.

Dave, "You ladies ready?"

Affirmative nods from the band.

"Everybody ready out there?" A loud cheer comes up from the crowd.

"1 2 3 4", the sound from the 2 electric guitars, tamed lightning; it crackles and sparks over the heads of the crowd. Bass guitar and drums right behind, setting the beat. The violin soars above it all.

The dance floor packed in an instant, a tangle of human movement, the music carrying the crowd. 30 seconds after the music starts, 3 men ask Sally to dance.

"Sally, dance?"

"I'd love to, if it's OK with the fella that brought me."

"Ah, . . . sure."

And so it went, every song, Sally danced. At 1 point, a line of 6 men, wait to dance with Sally. Trigby could have sold tickets.

Trigby watched as his date danced with every man in Long Beach; he could see why. *'Good golly, can this woman dance.'* Trigby's idea of dancing, a sedate country club fox-trot. *'I am so out of my league here.'*

And that's when it happened. Trigby realized there is a lot to Sally Mather, and he didn't know the half of it. He's been dating a demure schoolteacher, as if that is her entire life. *'I've got to up my game, in a big way.'*

After the first set, the band took a break and Sally sat down for the 1st time.

"Sally, you are an amazing dancer."

"Well thank you, Trigby. If you want to dance with me, you need to ask."

"I'd embarrass myself . . . and you."

"Trigby, all you need is to feel the music."

"Listen to the music?"

"No, feel the music, react to it, let it in. But you're right, you may need remedial training".

The second set begins. The songs are longer, Dave's solos more pronounced. Sally becomes more discriminating regarding dance partners. They didn't get a second dance if they can't keep up.

Trigby is in a totally new space, a wallflower. Leaning against the wall, watching Sally dance, Trigby thought again of what an amazing woman he had stumbled upon. And he realized he'd never heard music like this. And never, ever seen people dance like this. It's an athletic event; dancers twisting, twirling, dipping, swaying, shouting.

The dancers became part of the band, part of the music, part of the night.

"Wow." It is all Trig can say.

"Wow to you. I'm sorry I left you alone for so long; you're probably bored."

"Bored, no. Outclassed, yes."

"And, out danced."

"OK, Sally, here's my question: where did this music come from?"

"Out of the air. If you must call it something, call it American music. Dave writes lyrics and music. Most of what you have heard so far is his. With a few covers for effect. If you need a genre, which is always a mistake, it's 'Electrified Southern States & Chicago Negro Blues. Sung, played and written by a White boy."

"How do you know this, Sally? Who are you?"

"I'm a tall woman, with a sound mind, a modest bust, and a huge interest in good music."

"Wow. Sally, I didn't know any of this."

"I know, dear Trigby. Keep in mind, the things I know that you don't; it's a big number." Sally smiles as she says this.

The 3rd set begins with a slow blues crawler; Betsy takes the solo and soars. Dave answers her solo. Earlier in the night, Betsy played mostly rhythm guitar, staying in the background. She's abandoned that now, repeating Dave's guitar riff and then transforming it, adding her own bit. Same player, same instrument, played in a totally different way.

They are a team, Dave has been doing this forever; he leads Betsy, teaches her and more and more, lets her loose. They both look for a solo opening and whoever finds it 1st goes with it, hard. The other waits their turn, then responds, adding, changing. Dave and Betsy trade the lead back and forth.

Not to be outdone, the violin player is always there. Challenging Betsy and Dave for the leads, always playing hard, tense, leaning forward.

With leads constantly moving between 3 players, the beat; the forward movement of the songs and band, are in the hands of the rock-solid Fabulous 5 rhythm section – the bass guitarist and drummer.

"Listen now, Trigby. Listen to the drummer."

"The drummer?"

"Yes, Dixie, the drummer. You've been staring at her, with your mouth open all evening. Put your tongue back in and listen. Feel it."

Trigby had been caught. Yes, he'd been staring. Didn't realize it was that obvious. "OK, I'm listening.

"Those 1st sets, she's been playing behind the beat. Not on it, behind it. That gives the other players a little room. Now, in the 3rd set, she's playing ahead of the beat. If she doesn't, the other players go way, way out in the stratosphere, particularly Dave. He still leads the band, but in this set, the drummer, Dixie, holds the reins."

Trigby listened and watched. Dixie playing harder, taking control. Her long hair, fallen out of place, the pick gone, hair cascading over half her face. She takes gulps of air, holds her breath, plays through and then lets it out in a rush, taking another breath – perspiration on her forehead and upper lip.

"You're staring again, Trigby."

"No, no, . . . OK but I'm listening too. I get what you're saying; she's the boss."

"Maybe boss, but it's not the right word. She's more than that. She, Dave, Betsy and the rest of the band aren't just playing music; they are the music. And Dixie has control, for now, about where the music goes."

Like fine wine and great sex, the hum of the music ran on after the band stopped. There was a slight disruption when the house lights came on. "Good God, is this what we look like?"

Dave, God bless him, comes to the rescue. "Turn those damn lights down; they're women out there, think I'm good-looking."

Out in the night, on the sidewalk, the crazy, warm memory of the night and the music returned.

"Sally, I didn't know any damn thing about music before tonight."

"Glad you liked it, Trig."

That's when it hit Trigby; before he met Sally, he was one thing and now he is something else. Something newer, something better, something alive.

He should have told Sally this, but he couldn't put it into words. Looking at her, it seems she knows.

"Trigby, you don't have to go."

"I'm looking forward to seeing Dave. You taught me a lot last night."

"OK, but no whining when we get there."

The trip to Longview is longer, but the weather better. Tonight, Dave Martin and the band are playing at the VFW Hall. Trigby and Sally arrived early before the box office opened.

"We'll go around back and get in through the loading dock."

"Lead the way, Sally."

Dave and the Fab 5 are unloading their gear from a trailer hitched to a mile-long 1935 Cadillac 4-door sedan. It's 1 hell of a car!

"Nice car, Dave. I'm Trigby, a friend of Sally's."

"I can see that. Saw you last night hugging the wall like a ship out'a water."

The 2 men talked cars for a while and then Dave said he needed to start setting up.

"Can I help, Dave?"

"Hell yes, we gotta get everything in the trailer up on the stage." Dave picked up his guitar case and went inside.

'OK, I guess it means I need to get the gear out of the trailer and onto the stage.'

"Aw, come on Dave, did you con my man, Trigby, into unloading the trailer?"

"Not a con, more of an initiation."

"Well, initiate your way out to the trailer and help."

Trigby watched the show from backstage. He became Dave's assistant. "I left my acoustic guitar in the dressing room. I'll need it for the next song." Trigby got it for him. "I'm dying of thirst up here!" Trigby got Dave water. "Trig, tell that damn deaf sound man, to lower the volume on the violin or I'm gonna kill him." Trigby passed the request on to the sound man.

At the breaks, Trigby made sure Dave had water, food, and for the last break, liquor.

Seeing the show from backstage instead of the audience is striking. For one, the sound is better and gives a more accurate picture of the energy given off during a show. It also gave Trigby a closer look at Dixie, the drummer. Tonight, she is dressed in all white; hat, blouse, vest, trousers and boots. Her shining black hair loose, framing her face.

Trigby had helped Dixie set up her drum kit, breaking the *'Dixie spell'* for Trigby. He could look and talk to her without blushing. To his surprise, Dixie is a normal gal and friends with Sally. 3 hours later, the performance, with 2 encores, is over. The set list, a bit different than last night; new songs added, others deleted. There is a small backstage party; Trigby feels sorry for Dave and the Fab 5. They'd played well, giving and receiving energy from the crowd. Now the musicians, tired and spent, have the backstage hangers-on looking for more. They want autographs and photos; they want to be part of a bigger-than-life fantasy. Trigby received an adult dose of the traveling music scene and it didn't seem all that glamorous.

"Trigby, you passed the initiation; ready to hit the road with us?"

"Well, Dave, as tempting as your offer is, I'm good right where I'm at."

"Smart move. I hardly know you, but it seems you're a good man for Sally. Not sure you deserve her, but hell, what man does? I care for her, like I'm her big brother or something. So, if you're not good to her, I'll have to hurt you. And I'll probably get hurt myself, so for both of us, treat that woman right."

"I'm trying, Dave, I'm trying."

"Better do more than try; any gals in the band hear you treating Sally wrong, they'll beat the living shit out of you."

"Noted, Dave. I'll take care."

"Be sure you do. Now help get this gear back in the trailer."

CHAPTER 35

"Sally, where are we going and who are we going to see?"

"Astoria, to see the Clam Chorus at the Labor Temple."

"Clam Chorus, OK and what kind of music do they play? I know you hate this kind of question."

"Hate them, I do, but you keep asking. I'd say drunken, amplified folk/country music. But the important thing, it's good music."

The ferry ride across the Columbia adds to the evening. Being on the water at night, the sound of waves hitting the ferry, heading to the dark peninsula. The Labor Temple packed with people. Sally isn't so well known here; only half the crowd call her by name.

Her definition of the band's music; spot on. Most of the band seems to have had a couple of drinks beforehand, some; 4 or 5 drinks. It is good music, played at a loud volume. Music that is both old, from the hills and new, from the streets. Songs played great, as if the players needed to be snockered to play them this well. The lyrics match the music, a little slurred, a little sloppy, masking off-kilter, clever points of view; regarding love, life, politics and fear. In other words, the whole ball of wax rolled up in a messy, funny, revealing presentation. All of this with a beat you can dance to.

And dance she did. Sally danced in a different way tonight, loose like she'd had some drinks herself, but she hadn't. She's in sync with the spirit of the Clam Chorus. Trigby soaks it all in and loves it. The male guitarist/singer has a mole on his cheek, with long hairs growing out of it. He'd transformed this into a mustache on his cheek. Icky to look at but impossible to ignore. The female singer, right out of the Adams Family, looks like she's either going to a funeral or is the corpse. But, boy, can she sing.

On the way home, Sally and Trigby, holding hands, stand on the ferry deck, looking at the full moon rising over the River.

CHAPTER 36

Every time Trigby visits Naselle, he makes a point to visit the dishwasher at the Koffee Kup Kafé. The man doesn't recognize Trigby as the drunk that used to eat, sleep and drink Tokay wine in the alley. Trigby is OK with that. The dishwasher helped when he was down and almost out. It just seemed right to repay the man with a bit of respect and friendship.

Another of Trigby's haunts in Naselle is the 2nd Hand Store, across the street from the Koffee Kup. He hardly ever buys anything, just enjoys drifting through the store. A talkative wife and a quiet husband own the store. Trig spends a bit of time chatting with the wife and nods to the silent husband.

One fine spring day, the dishwasher and Trigby stood in the alley. The dishwasher on his break, smoking a cigarette. Trigby smoking his pipe. They'd been talking baseball when the discussion turned to the 2nd Hand Store. Trig learned a bit more about the 2nd Hand Store couple. A bit more than he needed to know.

The wife had been sick, off and on, for 2 years. In and out of the hospital several times and a couple of late-night runs to the emergency room. The husband loved his wife and hated her dog; they had no children. The wife put up with her husband and loved her tiny 14-year-old Chihuahua. The dog, nearly as sick as the wife.

The wife woke up during the night complaining she couldn't breathe.

"Rest quietly; I'll get you some water. Maybe it'll go away."

It didn't.

Next, the emergency room. Still, no help with the breathing and now her blood pressure sky high, weakening the heart.

"Your wife is nearing the end. We can't get her stable. You should prepare yourself. Now is the time to gather the family. You may have less than a day." The doctor's comments, efficient but kind.

"We don't have family left. It's just her and me. And the dog."

"I see; it could be hours but probably not more than a day. I'm sorry. The Chaplain will be coming to see you."

"Thank you, Doctor."

The husband had seen this coming, but it was still a shock. Activity is his remedy for grief. The first thing to handle, the dog. The poor thing had been incontinent for weeks and is vomiting on what seemed to be an hourly schedule.

At 9 am sharp, he is at the Veterinarian. The dog was euthanized later that morning. The husband had to admit he felt sad for the little bastard.

Next, his wife's things; the dresser first, the drawers emptied into grocery sacks. And then the dresses and coats in the closet went into two cardboard boxes. He took everything down to their 2nd Hand store.

When he got home, there was a call from the doctor.

"Your wife has made a remarkable recovery; heart rate is back to normal, blood pressure down and breathing unobstructed. Truly remarkable!"

After another two days in the hospital, the wife came home.

The couple are still married, still own the store and work together 6 days a week.

But things between them, never quite the same.

PART 10

CHAPTER 37

The idea of the decoy is Trigby's. With meat rationing and outrageous prices, all kinds of game are being shot out of season. Country folks complaining they can hear gunfire year-round. It turns out a lot of that gunfire is coming from the very same country folk.

Something must be done!

Trigby made the life-size 4-point buck decoy himself. He used wood, cotton wadding, covered with burlap sacking and a convincing shade of brown and white house paint. A taxidermist helped him with the head and horns. Somewhere along the line, Trigby got to calling the decoy Scruffy. Not sure why, but he liked it.

The downside to Scruffy is the weight. Scruffy weighs a ton. Well, maybe not a ton, but it takes both Trig and the Sheriff to get the damn thing in the Game Department's pickup. The standard joke is the amount of weight Scruffy has put on.

Driving around the county, Trigby looks for just the right spot. Usually, an open field ringed by trees, frequently marked with a 'No Trespassing' sign and sometimes a fence. If it isn't State land, he searches out the owner and asks permission. It is almost always given.

Trigby drives the truck out in the field, a good way from the road; Scruffy isn't as genuine close-up. He can wrestle Scruffy out of the truck alone, but the Sheriff will help Trig get the decoy back in the truck when the mission is done.

The truck is driven back to the road and hidden. Trig hides next, out of sight from the road, with a view of Scruffy and a view of the most likely areas a poacher would shoot from. With Scruffy and Trigby in place, it becomes a waiting game.

Trigby sits in his well-worn camp chair, binoculars on a cord around his neck and pipe handy; waiting for twilight. If he remembered to bring it, there is also a thermos of coffee. It's almost a formal process, kind of like a ceremony.

The tobacco pouch had been his father's, the lighter his grandfather's. The tobacco he smokes, a mixture of 3 different brands Trig buys twice a year in Longview. The amount of each brand in the pouch varies. Because he can't remember what ratio works best, sometimes Trigby enjoys smoking his pipe more than other times.

Pipe lit, coffee poured, Trig waits. He remembered another time, in the Army, when he was a different man. That man would have added rum to the coffee in the thermos. Added so much; it was like having a little coffee with your rum. And if in a rush, no coffee, all rum.

Trigby hadn't forgotten that man. He just didn't want to be him again.

A beat-up pickup pulls to the side of the road. 2 people get out. A man and a boy. Father and son. They look at the 4-point deer in the field. "Keep quiet, dammit, we don't want to spook it. Get my rifle off the rack. Billy, you try first."

Father and son climb over the fence and walk past the 'No Trespassing' sign. The son carefully aims and fires. The shot rings out through the field and into the trees. What they thought is a 4-point buck, doesn't move.

"Billy, you gone blind. First damn deer we have seen all day, right in front of us and you can't hit it. Shoot again." Same result.

"Now I'm not sure you're even my kin. Worst damn shooting I ever saw. Give me the rifle. Now".

The father takes 2 shots, same result. The 'deer' hasn't moved.

"What the hell is going on? I know I hit it."

As he raises the rifle to take a 3rd shot, Trigby, behind him, in a soft voice, says;

"Fellas, Scruffy won't die. You can keep firing at him all day; he'll still be standing. But you won't be doing that because you're under arrest."

CHAPTER 38

Sam Jacobs, the Sheriff of Wahkiakum County, seems to have been born for the office. A Deputy for several years and then elected to the position of Sheriff. A post he has held for 20 years. His manner is courtly, almost Southern gentleman, but born in the Northwest. Slight of stature, with a voice that is a tad high. As a Deputy, he was given the nickname 'Squeaky.' As in, "Squeaky, get off the damn radio; you're hurting my ears." Now he is referred to as Sheriff or Sir.

Those that dismiss Sam Jacobs, due to his manner or voice, do so at their own detriment.

Sam pulled the police cruiser into his mother's driveway.

"Dispatch, this is the Sheriff, show on code 7, next 20 minutes."

Sheriff Jacobs often took his coffee break at his Mom's house.

"Roger that, Sir."

Sam got out of the cruiser and stretched out his back, best he could. Debated whether to take his carry belt off and leave it in the car or keep it on. The belt carries his service revolver and ammunition, baton, tablet and pencil, hand cuffs, bear spray. *'Damn thing weighs a ton.'* Unfortunately, it's harder to take the belt off than to leave it on and bitch about it.

Sam opened the back porch door and went through to the kitchen. His mother, standing at the stove, had her back to him. "Hey Mom, what's cooking?" No response. "Mom, how are you doing?" This is a little louder. She replied, "I didn't hear you come in, dear." She didn't turn around. Sam went to her side, "Mom, how are . . . . what the hell happened?" Her right eye; a deep, mean purple.

"A misunderstanding. Its, its, . . . over now . . . . over. He didn't mean to . . ." The argument had been about the amount of time his mom, Gladys, spent on the phone. Now, Sam's stepfather, Bill, could hear Gladys talking, again. "If you're on that goddam phone, I'll. . ." Bill burst through the swinging door from the living room.

Sam stepped away from his mother and in a single stride, grabbed Bill by his collar and threw him, hard, up against the kitchen wall. Things are moving fast now. Too fast.

Before he realizes it, Sam has the barrel of his service revolver against Bill's temple.

A thought came to Sam from the back of his brain, '*slow down, slow down.'*

He had been taught never to point a gun at anyone unless he attended to use it. And never, ever, cock the trigger for the same reason.

'Slow down, slow down.'

Sam cocks the trigger. The sound is enormous.

"She, she . . . she was . . . "

The gun barrel moved from Bill's temple to his ear. "You sick son-of-a-bitch, you're telling me Mom's eye is her fault? Are you? Are you? Well, you're never gonna hurt her again. Ever."

"My ear, you're hurting, you're hurting me. I can't . . .," Bill, sobbing now.

"Bullet through that ear is gonna hurt worse."

'*Slow down, slow down.'* The thought moves to the front of his mind. Sam uncocks his revolver and put it back in the holster.

At almost the same moment, Gladys, in a calm, serious voice, said, "Sam dear, put the gun away; he's not worth it."

"You're right, Mom, you're right."

In an instant, the revolver is back in Bill's ear, cocked, ready to fire.

"But if I ever see, hear, or think you hurt my Mom again, I will shoot you dead."

One might think this encounter would lead to awkward Thanksgiving and Christmas dinners. But it didn't; everyone got along; Bill a perfect, if a bit timid, husband. Gladys, his loving wife. This day is never brought up, although Sam made sure that he sat across from his stepfather at every family dinner and stared at him for overly long moments.

CHAPTER 39

"Do you like jazz, Trigby?"

"Maybe, do you like it?"

"Yes, very much."

"Sally, I love jazz."

"Good, we're going to Astoria to hear some good jazz."

The club, if you could call it that, is in the basement of the M & N Building in downtown Astoria. The club is at the back of the building; the entrance is from the below sidewalk level, gravel parking lot. It is a tiny, smoky place with a door, no windows, 4 tables and a dozen chairs. Someone's dining room table serves as a bar, there isn't a stage and the club doesn't have a liquor license. The owners, a Negro couple, newcomers from Portland, serve ridiculously high-priced club soda and ginger ale as refreshments. But if a patron happens to bring a flask (or 2), that is their business.

"Hi Winnie, this is my friend Trigby."

"Trigby, that is the whitest name in the whole damn world. If you're a friend of Sally's, you must be OK. What are you drinking?"

"2 ginger ales and ice."

Sally and Trigby are lucky enough to get a table. Winnie brings the drinks; ginger ales in bottles and 2 glasses filled with ice.

"You get both ginger ales, Trig; I'll just have a little bit."

With the ease and grace of a magician, Sally draws a discrete silver flask filled with gin out of her pocket. She pours gin on top of the ice and returned the flask to her pocket without looking at either.

"I'll top it off with a smidge of ale, if you don't mind, Trigby."

Sally knows Trigby doesn't drink and why. She doesn't drink much or often, but she will on certain occasions. Trigby doesn't mind and neither does Sally.

"Sally, before they start, can I get a bit of info regarding jazz? I'm hoping to score well in my music appreciation class."

"Trying to be the teacher's pet?"

"If you must know, trying to pet the teacher and more."

"Good luck with that. Jazz is about improvisation. There's usually a melody in the beginning; that's what the band improvises on. The lead players bounce their take on the tune around for a while. Passing the lead back and forth. Sometimes the bass player and drummer get a solo. The bass solo, always dull, the drum solo usually dull, but in this case, the kid on the drums can swing, big time!"

The band is a pickup band with players from Astoria and Portland. Saxophone and trumpet, Portland. Bass and drums, Astoria. The players from Portland, Negroes. From Astoria, White. The drummer, a white boy who looks about 14 years old.

The sax player counts off the time, drummer picks it up with brushes, bass follows. Sax plays the melody and the trumpet picks it up. The music is dreamy, surprisingly lush. Sax and trumpet, the stars of the show. The drummer keeps time, not a beat; this isn't a sound that will knock you off your chair and onto the dance floor. This is music to float away on.

Trigby, a little antsy in the beginning, gets into it. He focuses on the interplay between sax and trumpet; it is understated and entertaining. In the 2nd set, he listens to the drummer, *'man-o-man, can that kid play!'* Then the bass gets Trigby's attention.

"Hey, teacher," Trigby says in a whisper.

"Yes, my randy student, if this is more about petting, hold off until after the show."

"What? No. Me? I've been listening to the bass. He's playing a different song."

"I know. Interesting, isn't it?"

Winnie walked over to Trigby and gave him a look that said, *'Shut up or get out!'*

But Trigby is right; the bass plays a different song on almost every song. Different, but not distracting. It mixes with what the rest of the band is playing and makes it better.

The music ends around midnight after an outstanding solo from the 14-year-old drummer. There was no bass solo.

CHAPTER 40

The drummer, Tommy, is not 14 years old; he is 15. And a protegee in percussion. When he was 9, he played drums in the junior high school band, at 12 in the high school orchestra and at 14, percussion in the county orchestra. Now he plays wherever he wants. The only place he can't play is bars, due to his age.

His most maturing venue, musically and in other ways, was at the Eagles Hall in Long Beach, Washington.

The gig was for a 4-piece bar band, backing another performer. Due to a 30-day stretch in the county slammer, the band is missing the drummer after his 5th drunk driving charge. One of the band members knows Tommy and his talent. Got him on the phone and Tommy asked his parents if he could play across the river in Long Beach. With approval from his parents, Tommy had his drum kit sitting on the sidewalk when the band's van picked him up.

On the ferry over, Tommy asked the obvious question, "where are we playing?"

"Eagles Hall."

"Doesn't the Eagles have a bar in it? How am I going to get in?" Tommy is a conservative kid, from a conservative family. Whatever the situation, he wants to do right and not get in trouble.

"There is a room downstairs they use for these occasions."

"What occasions?"

"Don't worry Tommy; you are playing and getting paid."

The room downstairs is much smaller than the hall upstairs. But it has a stage and a bar. The bar doesn't concern Tommy anymore. *'What are they going to do, arrest me?'* He hopes to snag his 1st beer tonight.

The band got to the Eagles at 5:30PM, were set up and drinking beer (everybody but Tommy) by 6. The show, scheduled to start at 8.

"How come we're so early?" Tommy asks.

"Need to rehearse with the performer beforehand. You'll have a big part in how this goes, so pay attention."

As it turned out, nobody had to worry about 15-year-old Tommy, paying attention.

The musicians ran through the playlist for half an hour. Tommy knew most of the tunes and plays so well he faked the ones he didn't know. After the last song, a woman came on the stage. Her face, heavily made up, rings on all her fingers, high heels, wearing a bathrobe. The bathrobe didn't make sense to Tommy. And no microphone set up for her, obviously the singer.

"OK boys, play my intro," the woman said in the sexiest voice Tommy had ever heard.

After the song, "Great, nicely done. Hey drummer, how old are you?"

"Old enough," this from the self-appointed leader of the band.

"Right, play the 2nd song; that's my entrance, play it loud." The band hit it and she came out from the wings, moving in a sensual dance. Particularly sensual for a woman in a bathrobe. 2 more songs, each with a slightly different dance. The bathrobe seems to be hampering her. She takes it off. Except for 2 small flowers on her breasts and a tiny triangle of cloth below, she is naked.

"Holy smokes!" Tommy could feel the red flush move up his face. Sweating so much, his drumsticks slid out of his

hand. Bending down to retrieve them he knocked over his cymbal set.

"Hey, drummer, what's your name?" No more sexy voice.

"Tommy."

"OK Tommy, you call me Miss Devine."

"Yes, Miss . . . . Miss . . . . . Devine."

"Good. We are both working here. I get paid for my erotic dancing and you for drumming. Do you understand?"

"Yes, Miss Devine."

"Good. Neither of us will get paid, if you can't play the drums."

"I can do it; I can play!" There is no way, no way Tommy is going to miss this.

"Excellent. Start from the top." Miss Devine kept her robe off.

After a complete run-through, she is satisfied with the band, especially the drummer. Tommy managed it by playing with his eyes closed.

"Very good, Tommy. You're the best player in this group." Miss Devine said this over her shoulder to the rest of the band as she stood facing Tommy. The robe remained off. "Now we come to my grand finale."

"On the last song, I'll turn my back to the audience, take off these roses and hand them to you. Keep your eyes on my eyes, Tommy or you won't make it."

Tommy took the roses.

"Your eyes on my eyes, Tommy."

"Yes, Miss Devine."

"Then you will hand me these." She gave Tommy 2 bright tassels with small suction cups. She attached the tassels to her breasts. "And give me the roses back; I'll throw them to the crowd at the end of the show. Are you with me Tommy?"

"Yes."

"OK, as I turn back to the audience, you start a drum roll. When I get the tassels going, hit the bass drum, hard. Then keep in time to the tassels."

"But I won't be able to see the tassl___."

"I know that Tommy, just as well. Watch my hips, the boobs stay stationary. The tassels are powered by hip movement. Once I get them going fast, I'll put my hands behind my head like this. And the shows over."

Tommy's eyes almost popped out of his head. He kept eye contact with Miss Devine but utilized his peripheral vision to the maximum. His eyes; the size of pie plates.

"Got it, Tommy?"

"Yes, I do!"

"How about you gu__." She said this as she turned around to the rest of the band members. "Hey, eyes up! How about you guys? You got it?"

"Yep, yes, yes."

The show went well. The drunk and fairly wild crowd loved Miss Devine; they couldn't have cared less about the band. The manager paid the band and Miss Devine in cash. She was in her dressing room.

"Thanks, Johnny, see you in 2 months. If you see my drummer, please send him back and get me 2 shots of Jack Daniels and a beer chaser."

Tommy went to the dressing room door and knocked.

"Hi Tommy, come on in. Have a beer."

Without the make-up and clothed, Tommy almost didn't recognize her.

"Thanks, Miss Devine."

"Miss Devine, all for the show, Tommy. Now I'm just Beverly; call me Bev."

This night, for a 15-year-old male, in the 1940's, from little Astoria, Oregon, is as good as it gets.

CHAPTER 41

Trigby became a regular at the 2nd Hand Store in Naselle. Sally, also a frequent shopper at the store, she has good luck finding phonograph records there. Trigby started looking for records at the store as well. He wants to show Sally that he too has an interest in music.

He'd become a fan of the store and its owners. Knowing their back story, Trigby is fascinated by the couple. The wife a talker, the husband quiet, reserved. The 2 have definite roles and zones in the store. Wife at the front; greets everyone that comes in and talks their ears off. Husband at the back, rearranging the stock. Slowly, carefully, silently. When he is done, everything looks pretty much the same.

The items in their 2nd Hand Store are a mixture of things, a lot of things. Ranging from the graceful to the grotesque, beautiful to ugly. Prices for everything, amazingly cheap. Trigby can't imagine how they make a living. He bought a rather large painting for Lawson's living room. The picture scared the Lawson's daughter, Jenny. Mrs. Lawson said if they had an outhouse, it would be appropriate in there. Pastor Lawson thanked Trigby and, the next week, set it on fire in the burn barrel.

Today, Trig, is in Naselle at the 2nd Hand Store looking for more records. He didn't have any luck. The best he can find is a 12-record Beethoven set featuring the London Symphony Orchestra. Not what he's looking for.

He saw a set of golf clubs and a golf bag. He'd had a fine set of Rawlings clubs; they might still be at the Astoria Country Club. But this mismatched set; woods, irons and 2 putters from 4 different manufacturers suited Trigby just fine.

"Jenny, want to learn how to play golf?"

"No, thank you, Trigby."

"Great, let's get started."

"Trigby, I don't think I would be good at golf."

"Perfect, we'll play for money."

"1st, we'll make you some clubs." Trigby cut down a 6-iron for Jenny and 1 of the putters. For some unknown reason, there is a 7-wood as part of the set, that gets shortened as well.

"I need more clubs, Trigby. Can you make the rest of them my size?"

"How about you learn to play with these to start?"

Trigby taught Jenny how to wrap grips on her 3 clubs.

The grassy area between the ball field and the parsonage became their practice range.

"If you hit my house or worse, break a window, I will wrap a golf club around your neck. Do you understand me, Jenny? Trigby?"

They both understood the risk they were taking with Helen Lawson.

The next morning. "Trigby, I'm dropping off Teddy; I can't be late for the school bus."

"OK, Jenny, I'm heading out myself. Put Teddy in the truck . . . and hey, you'd better run to catch that bus."

Teddy is Jenny's dog before and after school. During the day, he is Trigby's dog. It's like his own security detail. The dog follows Trig everywhere. To the diner for coffee, to the diner for lunch. At the office, if Trig goes to the restroom, Teddy acts as a blockade at the restroom door. If the 2 are in the field, Teddy sits upright in the passenger seat, nose out the half-open window, alert, watching. It's like the dog is the patrol officer and Trigby merely the escort driver.

Today the Teddy/Trigby squad heads out on the backroads, North of Grays River. Complaints of night shooting, trapping and moonshining have been coming in from the area, particularly on Snag Road. An hour is spent on that road and its side roads. Every now and again, a glimpse of Hogs Creek is visible. No sign of trapping or trespassing. Night shooting would have to wait till dusk. But a series of stills are found halfway down an abandoned logging road, beside the creek. It is Teddy, the dog, that finds the stills.

Trigby figured he deserved a break. Suffering from what he called *'tired butt.'* The horrible driver's seat and bad shocks make the Jeep awful to drive for more than an hour. Teddy leapt from the truck and surveyed the general area. Trigby got out as well; stretched, poured himself a cup of coffee, lit his pipe.

This is a part of the job Trig cherished; out in the woods, peaceful, a period to relax. Thankful for quiet. Except his partner is making one hell of a racket. Trigby hadn't noticed where the dog headed off to, but he could hear him crashing around in the woods.

"Teddy, come." No response. "Teddy, Come!" No response. "Dammit, dog, get over here." No response.

Well . . . there could be a couple of things going on. Teddy could have a small animal cornered, a porcupine, bad for the dog or maybe a skunk, bad for the dog and Trigby.

Trig finished his coffee, knocked out the embers from his pipe and fought through the underbrush toward the ruckus. 15 minutes later, with a rip in the backside of his trousers and a deep scratch on his cheek, Trigby can't see Teddy but knows he is close. That's when his feet gave way and he started sliding on his butt, down a steep, muddy embankment. When he landed in it, Hogs Creek stopped his sliding. Wet, cold, dirty and looking like he'd been in the wilderness for a decade, Trigby felt a bit ornery toward his canine partner. He heard the dog downstream and since he was already wet and the sides of the canyon left no other way to proceed, Trigby slipped and sloshed down the creek.

After 100 yards or so, the canyon broadened and there was a still and Teddy. The dog is lapping at something on the ground. Either the still is abandoned, or the moonshiners are wildly messy. Bottles and trash littered the site. Trigby picked up a bottle, took a sniff and knew it was corn liquor, which Teddy seemed to enjoy. Luckily, Trigby brought a leash, and he moved Teddy away from the spillage and leashed him to a tree.

So . . . now Trigby had new problems. A still, and what to do about it; a possibly drunk dog and how to get back to the road. The dog contained for the moment and the solution to the still, solved. A rusty ax sat next to a few pieces of firewood. Trigby used it to smash every bit of smashable glass and copper parts of the still. Teddy barking as if to say, 'Hey I wasn't done with that!"

Trigby had a hunch and it turned out right. This still is the 1st of 3; the next is 150 yards downstream. He dispatches it with the ax. Following a path up from the creek is the last site. Trigby lays waste with the ax. Apparently, the plan was not to have all the workings in 1 place. At each site, he searches for any evidence that could point to the distillers. Trigby can't find anything. Most moonshiners don't leave business cards lying around.

When you are wet, cold and miserable, a Willys Jeep offers no comfort. Teeth chattering, Trigby drives home. Teddy did not sit upright in the passenger seat; he lay on the floor of the Jeep, sound asleep.

That night, dinner at the Lawsons.

"Good Lord! What happened to you?" This from Everett.

"You should have seen me before I showered and changed my clothes."

"Yikes, Trigby, what happened to your cheek? Did another woman punch you?"

"No, Jenny, my current injuries are due to your drunk dog."

Next morning, coffee at the café.

"Hi Trigby, where's your dog?"

"Sleeping off a hangover, Mandy."

"Sleeping off wha____. What happened to your cheek?"

Arnold, the veterinarian, slipped into the café.

"Let me look at your cheek. How did this happen?"

"Morning, Arnold, happened while I wrestled an anaconda."

Luckily for Trigby, Sam Jacobs, the County Sheriff, walked in. Saving Trigby another 15 minutes of questions and then 30 minutes of ribbing.

"Morning Sam, get your coffee to go. I need to take you to a 3-still moonshine set-up."

"Great, is it up and running?"

"Nope, Sam, in a true act of inter-agency cooperation, I demolished all 3 sites."

"OK, but next time leave them up. I can usually tell the moonshiner by the way he sets the still."

"You're welcome, Sheriff. Get your coffee and let's go; we're taking your cruiser."

Luxuriating in the Dodge police cruiser, with huge seats, all the latest cop-car gadgets, and a heater, Trigby watched the rain come down in buckets. He knew a man of the Sheriff's temperament would not enjoy traipsing up a creek in a rainstorm. Trigby took the Sheriff to the 3rd still site only.

"Thanks for your help, Trigby. I appreciate it. Just from the amount of junk spread out, I'm pretty sure who the 'shiners' are. The Nelson boys. Might arrest them for felony littering as much as moonshining. Never drink any of their shine, might not see again."

The picture of Teddy lapping it up flashed into Trigby's mind.

"On the way back, I'm gonna try a couple of side roads. Just want to make sure the Nelsons don't have other sites."

"Did that yesterday, Sheriff. Didn't find anything."

"No offense, Trigby, but this is a crafty bunch. Plus, can't have the Game Warden doing all my work."

Another 45 minutes of driving rough roads. The Chevy took it all without a problem. Hell, Trigby could ride around all day in this luxury.

"What is that over there, Sheriff? That open patch."

"Golf course. I think we are done; the Nelsons either retired or moved on."

"Golf course? Way out here?"

"Well, old golf course. Supposed to be part of a hunting lodge, resort, big deal. Golf course, all that got built. Pretty much abandoned now."

The parsonage is getting to be in Jenny's range. She could hit the house with a well-hit shot and the right wind conditions. Trigby remembered Helen's warning. She would never harm her child. But Trigby isn't her child; he'd take the blame. And the 7-wood wrapped around his neck.

A trip to the old golf course became a weekly endeavor for Trigby, Jenny and Teddy. In the beginning, they played 'pail golf.' At what might be the 1st tee, Jenny and Trigby each hit shots from a pail filled with 2nd Hand Store used golf balls, until the pail was empty. Then they'd walk, picking up balls. Once the pail became full again, they'd hit balls until it was empty.

Next came 'best ball golf.' Trigby would tee off, then Jenny would tee off from a spot Trigby chose, a good way down the fairway. If Jenny hit a good shot, her ball could pass his and become the 'best ball'. Trigby would hit the best ball and the whole procedure would begin again. So, the 'best ball' is based on distance, playability and the fact they could find the damn ball. Amazing how often Jenny had the 'best ball.'

With a bit of research, Trigby found that due to unpaid taxes, the county owned the golf course. With more diligence, he found an egg rancher whose property adjoined the course, had been mowing it a couple of times a year. Jenny gave the farmer a bouquet of wildflowers as a thank you. The gift caused the farmer and his wife to be smitten by this wonderful child. Particularly compared to their own children, they saw once a year, on a good year.

After the next bouquet, Jenny received a dozen eggs in return. Which caused a return gift of Helen Lawson's famous chocolate cake. Helen and Everett Lawson went to see the course. Helen soon became fast friends with the farmer's wife. Everett, in his no pressure, sincere way, invited the couple to church. And they came! Sheriff Sam Jacobs would come out occasionally, not to play golf, just for the walk. Turns out he is a master at finding lost golf balls. His 3-pail day is a record that won't likely be broken.

"I started this to teach the kid golf. Now it's turned into a parade!" Sure, Trigby could privately grumble but he enjoyed getting his share of the free, non-rationed eggs. Which he gave to Sally, who wanted to see what this golfing thing was all about.

"I was co-captain of the Women's Longview Community College Golf Team."

Trigby wasn't sure if he should salute.

On Saturday, Trigby, Jenny and Teddy picked up Sally and her dog Sandy for a round of 'dog golf.' Sally laid a towel down first and then put her leather golf bag in the bed of the Game Warden pickup, along with her dog. Each club, snuggled in a leather cover with embroidered club number. She has sunglasses and a plaid visor, which match her golf outfit. She carries a leather satchel, matching her head covers and club bag.

"Holy Smokes, Trigby, we should've dressed up!" Jenny whispered.

"Hi Trigby, Jenny."

"Hi to you gorgeous, what are you carrying?"

"Golf shoes." Trigby knew they would match the rest of her ensemble.

"Where did you get the wonderful bag?" Jenny asked.

"My parents gave me the clubs and bag when I graduated. Dad said it cost more than his truck."

"Should we warm up first, Trigby? Is there a driving range?"

"Actually, no. This course doesn't have greens, much less a driving range." For Trigby and Jenny, 'warming up' meant getting the clubs out of the back of the truck and releasing the hounds.

After more than a few practice swings, Sally is ready.

"Where do we tee off?"

"Anywhere you'd like."

"Where are you teeing off from, Trigby?"

"Right here." He over-swung a bit, but it is a powerful shot down the right side, ending up just outside the fairway. If there was a fairway.

"Jenny starts further up the course."

"I'll start from here."

From just her set-up, Trigby knows he is in trouble. With a graceful take-away, the club passed parallel to the ground on the back swing. And then a completely unrushed swing, the ball flying down the nonexistent fairway. Not as far as Trigby's shot, but a beautiful thing to see.

Trig picked out a place for Jenny to shoot from and she hit a good shot, straight, just past Trigby's ball. It became the 'best ball.' Jenny hit her best ball, another nice shot;

straight, short of the green. Next, Sally hit from the same spot; the ball landed on what used to be a green. The pin, a tree branch stuck in the ground, 15 feet away from her ball.

Trigby hit a nice shot from the same place that went well past the green.

"Should I be keeping my score? Are there score cards?"

"No cards. Jenny keeps the score in her head. And the rules."

"Not many rules," Jenny says.

"OK, so with no putting, how do we score this hole, Jenny?"

"If you could putt it, Miss Mather, how many putts to get in the cup?"

"Maybe 2 or 3."

"That's a lot, Miss Mather."

"Not from 15 feet."

"Sally, Sally, we have faith in you. Score it as a 1-putt. Total 3 for the hole."

"So, a par Trigby?"

"Nope, an eagle." Trigby and Jenny said this in unison.

"This is the shortest par 5 in the world."

"It was a par 3, but we raised it. Trigby's idea. We raised all of them to 5's. It sure helped our scoring."

"I'll bet it did, Jenny. So, as a team, we are 2 under par after 1 hole. Are there any other rules I should know about?"

"Only 2 rules. If you hit a bad shot, you can put the ball where you meant it to go. No penalty."

"OK, what is the other rule?"

"No bad words."

"Good rule. Is there a penalty?"

"1 penny, every bad word. You have to pay the other player."

"Great rule, Jenny. How many pennies do you have?"

"97."

"And you, Trigby?"

"None."

PART 11

CHAPTER 42

The need for and lack of explosives became a problem. Jukka's problem.

The Germans were to secure it and transport it to Naselle. Then they weren't, then they were and, in the end, they couldn't. 4 different weeks-long delays. Next, the Japanese got involved. The submarine carrying the explosives sank mid-Pacific.

Now the lowest person on the top-secret mission totem pole, is in charge of securement.

"If we do not have the explosives within 48 hours, I will have my men secure it on their own. After they weight your body with chains and drown you in that miserable river."

"The delay is not my doing. I know where the explosives are; I'm waiting on the 1-ton truck to bring them here. The truck is Aberdeen's responsibility."

"Regardless of responsibility, if not delivered in 48 hours, you drown."

The truck arrived the next day.

Jukka had found the explosives needed at a quarry outside of Cathlamet. He'd applied for a job there, got a tour of the site and was offered employment. Jukka said he would think about it and never went back.

The raid began at midnight; Jukka and 8 storm-troopers drove the truck to the quarry. The quarry is up a remote country road, nearest neighbor 3 miles away. A trooper driving, the truck moved to an 8-foot high, padlocked gate. In the lowest gear, the truck inched forward: the gate proved no match for a 1-ton truck.

Next, the warehouse doors. The roll-up door appears to be locked from the inside. A regular-sized door sat beside the roll-up. A brief discussion ensues regarding breaching the door. Kick it in, shoot the lock, use a crowbar? Jukka takes a more direct approach. He turns the doorknob, and the door opens.

Roll-up doors opened from inside and the truck drove in. The explosives were loaded and the truck left. Total time for the raid, not counting transport, 12 minutes.

Explosives, troopers and truck made it back to the Naselle house without incident. The barn became a bomb factory, explosives carefully placed into water-proof containers, sealed and then repacked into the truck.

Everything ready and waiting. Men, explosives, transport; waiting for tides and shipping schedules.

Trigby is early for the 10AM coffee at Mandy's Cafe. Chats and teases the waitress/owner Mandy. Their dialogue is familiar and light-hearted. Sam Jacobs, the sheriff of Wahkiakum County, arrives at the same time as Fire Chief Lenard Larsen.

"I got a helluva phone call this morning, 6AM!" Sam Jacobs says this before he gets his coffee. "Some jackass stole a helluva lot of high explosives from the quarry behind Cathlamet. Had to have a big truck; the quarry is still trying to figure out how much was stolen. I just got back."

"Somebody's planning on blowing something up. Something big."

"I'm thinking the same thing, Trigby and it scares the shit out of me."

Jukka, after paying, left the rooming house. He didn't plan on coming back. Sitting in the Ford pickup truck generously given by his superiors, Jukka waits in line for the ferry. A SS officer had once told him, 'Before going into battle, get your mind straight.' Jukka's mind is straight. He is doing duty to his country and Fuhrer. By doing so, he is leaving behind a promising career, a town and lifestyle he likes and a woman he loves. He does realize those feelings are not reciprocated by the woman.

He got the explosives needed; he will bring them to the site on the River. Next, boats and crew to the designated site. In other words, Jukka will do everything required for this mission. After the mission, he will not be returning to Astoria or Germany. He will have done his duty and will do no more.

Veiko walked into his house, slammed the front door closed, turned around, opened the door and went back outside, slamming the front door again. He paced back and forth on the small porch, trying to light his pipe and failing. Cursing in Finnish, Veiko grabbed the unlit pipe from his mouth and threw it as far as he could. It bounced down the long flight of stairs and onto the street.

And that made Veiko madder. He threw the front door open again and marched inside, slamming the door behind him.

Helmi is getting mad too. "Veiko, you slam that door 1 more time and I slam your head with this skillet. What is the matter with you?"

Veiko couldn't answer, too mad. Tried to answer a couple of times but couldn't. Helmi went back to the kitchen with the skillet and came back with a bottle of Aquavit and a glass. She poured out a serious amount and Veiko tried to drink it all in 1 gulp. He started coughing and couldn't stop. The coughing took some of the anger out of him.

"I am mad at Jukka. Mad, very mad at him. After all I have done!"

"Veiko, Veiko, calm down. What did he do?"

"Did not show up for fishing today."

Veiko is right to be mad; hard to fish without a mate. Almost impossible. Veiko tried, it did not go well. He would get a small length of net onboard and stop the winch. Pick the salmon out of the net and throw them into the locker. Bring the empty net to the stern of the boat, then race to the bow and bring more net aboard. Hard work; slow and laborious.

Missing a day of fishing was one big thing but not giving notice to the skipper is another, much bigger thing. No call from Jukka, no note from Jukka. As Veiko thought:

"Ei mitaan".
'No nothing.'

And that was it. It is like Jukka had disappeared, vanished from sight and then from the mind. At first, Veiko, Helmi and Dea were concerned, distraught. And then angry, the women not as angry as Veiko. Then Veiko found another mate; not as young, not as hard-working, not as capable as Jukka. But competent and dependable.

The considerable space that Jukka had taken up in these 3 lives began to close. And then, like Jukka, it disappeared.

CHAPTER 43

They left in the middle of the night.

Commander Hann, like his troops, is more than ready to go. The small cottage and out-buildings became like a prison. Fighting men need to be fighting or moving to fight. Waiting, under cover, out of sight, is a spy's life, not a warrior's life.

All the boats, explosives and troops moved out earlier in the week. All that remained are Commander Hann, Assistant Commander Giese and Jukka. They are the last to leave.

"Are the barn and buildings ready, Giese?"

"Yes, Oberstrum Hann, kerosene throughout, explosives and timers ready to go." This will be a diversion for what is to happen at the River.

"Set timers for 40 minutes and bring the truck around."

On the way to the launch site on the River, the 3 heard a muffled explosion and stopped to see flames coming from the house and barn on Parpilla Road. The flames lit up the sky.

The plans for the strikes on Liberty ships had been long and tense. Commander Hann and Jukka made many trips to Aberdeen. On his 1st trip, the Commander hated everyone he met. These are not fighting men; they are bureaucrats, delegators, pencil pushers. Given a choice, the Commander would have shot them all.

Jukka had to listen to the complaints for the entire 2 ½ hour ride home. There were strong hints the Commander didn't hold Jukka in high regard either.

The decisions made at meetings included how many Liberty ships must be sunk to choke the shipping channel, information flow from the Kaiser shipyards, escape plans for the troopers after the attack. And a hundred more issues.

One sticking point is the Japanese must agree to all of the plans. This took time, a lot of time. How the various plans got to Japan for discussion is a mystery to the Commander. Why they needed to be sent is also a mystery.

"Jukka, why should we need their approval? They delivered us here, thank them very much. Now we need their approval on every detail? Horseshit. We move and we move fast. The longer we wait on them, the greater chance we take. Yes, we, those on the ground. Those willing to give their blood and lives for the Fatherland."

"I agree, Commander."

Jukka stopped listening after the 3rd trip to Aberdeen.

What the Commander knew, but the leaders in Tokyo, Berlin and even Jukka did not seem to know, the 1st casualty of war is planning.

Hann, Giese and Jukka turned off the paved Highway 4 onto the graveled Hemsley Road.

"Mind the odometer; the main force is 7 kilometers ahead." The final planning for tonight had taken time, effort and patience. Patience is something Hann had a lack of to begin with and now there is none left.

3 kilometers in, there are lookouts posted on both sides of the road. Well hidden, invisible, heavily armed, with 2 ground mounted machine guns, long rifles and side-arms. These weapons are to be used only as a last resort. But no local vehicle is to come down Hemsley Road.

2 kilometers further is the Command Center. Double ring security, medics and exit vehicles; fueled up, ready to go the moment the mission is over. Everything has been done to make the Command Center invisible.

Camouflaged, defensive positions manned, no lights, no fires, cold rations.

The collapsible boats are hidden at the River's edge; 8 hp outboard motors attached, explosives onboard. The River calm, no wind. Sky dark, no moon.

"Are the Liberty Ships on schedule?"

"Yes, Oberstrum Hann. Left Kaiser Boat Yards at 01:15. Estimated to pass here at 02:20."

"I want boats on the water at 02:05."

"Yes, Sir."

This hushed conversation took place at the River's edge, a ½ kilometer from the command center.

In a small community like Wahkiakum County, when there is a major fire, it's all hands-on-deck. 1st call went out to the county volunteer fire crew and next the Sheriff, State Patrol, Game Warden and anybody else that could help.

The cities of Long Beach, Ilwaco and Naselle sent fire trucks and crew to the fire. The trucks were a blessing; 3 trucks pumping water from the Naselle River cut the fire down quickly. By the time Trigby and the Sheriff got to the scene, there are fire crews, fire trucks, fire hoses and half of the male population from 2 counties fighting the dying flames.

"Well, Trig, they need us like a rowboat with no oars."

"I agree, Sheriff. Let's head back. I was in the middle of a great dream; maybe I can reconnect to it."

"Trigby, that's something I can't do. Once I'm up, I'm up. Heard about the Gaffke's poaching deer between Highway 4 and the River. Probably up by Hemsley Road. Thought I'd check it out. Might need help."

And I might need some more shut eye. "Sure, Sheriff, glad to help."

"Thanks, Trigby."

A Ford truck, new during the Coolidge administration, pulled up. Bright, high headlights on.

"Dammit, turn those lights out."

"Just need to know who I'm dealing with." Bill Young, the ex-game warden, slowly exercised his way out of the truck. "I wanted to fight the fire, is it out?"

Bill got the full run-down. "Damn, hate to miss a big fire. But I'll do a little night reconnaissance with you if you want."

"Glad to have you along, Bill. Let's take my cruiser so it doesn't look like a darn parade. Might need a little more firepower. Put any weapons you got in my trunk."

Bill opened the trunk, "who are you planning on fighting, Sheriff? You got enough ordinance back here to start another war."

"Preparedness is important."

Turning off Highway 4, the cruiser took Hemsley Road toward the River.

"You might want to stop here, Sheriff," Trigby said. All 3 men get out, flashlights pointing straight down.

The road, rarely used, is crisscrossed with tire tracks. "Odd, this much traffic."

"I'm thinking the same thing, Trigby. The Gaffke's have 1 broken down Ford."

"Well, this is a lot more than a pickup. Look at these tracks here; that's a 1-ton truck, with a heavy load."

"Command, Command - Position 1 reporting. Polizei- oder Militärfahrzeug auf der Straße."

"Command, Command - Position 1 reporting. Police or military vehicle on the road."

"Position 1 – Beschreiben Sie das Fahrzeug.

"Position 1 – Describe the vehicle."

"Befehl, Automobil. 4 Türen. Insignien an der Tür. 3 Insassen, die keine Uniformen tragen."

"Command, automobile. 4 doors. Insignia on the door. 3 occupants, not wearing uniforms."

"Position 2 – Bericht - Sehen Sie ein Fahrzeug?"

"Position 2 – Report - Do you see a vehicle?"

"Ich habe meine Position in Richtung Straße verschoben. Ja, ich sehe ein Fahrzeug, 3 Männer, Lichter leuchten auf den Boden."

"I have moved my position toward the road. Yes, I see a vehicle, 3 men, lights shining down to the ground."

"Trigby, do you hear something?"

"I did. Something over there. Thought I heard talking."

"Bill, get my shotgun out of the trunk. I'm gonna put a little light on the subject." The Sheriff got in the cruiser, turned on the searchlight, directing it on the forest. The night became day in the beam of light.

"Position 1 zum Befehl. Sie sind bewaffnet und haben ein Licht auf meine Position."

"Position 1 to Command. They are armed and have a light on my position."

"Vorrücken oder Rückzug?"

"Advancing or retreating?"

"Voranschreiten."

"Advancing."

"Feuer nach Belieben."

"Fire at will."

Bill Young stands in the middle of the road. "DAMMIT, WHOEVER IS OUT THERE, SHOW YOURSELF." Bill bellows this, shattering the quiet of the night.

"Bill, pipe down and get yourself behind the cruiser."

"IF YOU ARE THE DAMN GRAFFKE'S, GET YOUR ASS OUT HERE BEFORE I COME IN AN . . ."

The rip of machine gun fire is a distinct, deadly sound. Bill Young hit the ground hard, the Sheriff and Trigby crouching down, using the cruiser for cover.

"ARE YOU SHOOTING AT ME? SON-A-BITCH BASTARDS." Bill now up with 2 blasts from his shotgun. "SHERIFF, TRIGBY, GIVE SOME COVER FIRE." Bill reloads, walking backward. Fires 2 shots, reloads, 2 more shots.

Trigby and the Sheriff, popping up from behind the cruiser, looking for the muzzle flash from the forest to return fire. "I'M COMING IN HOT," bellowed Bill. And he is coming in hot; limping, trying to run, cursing as he dives behind the cruiser.

"The bastards shot me in the damn foot." Bill's hunting boot shows a neat circle in the side, blood oozing out.

The Sheriff manages to crawl into the cruiser and use his radio. "Fort Columbia, this is Sheriff Sam Jacobs, Wahkiakum County. I am under heavy fire, on Hemsley Road, from 1 or more shooters. Heavy, rapid-fire. I need help from all available agencies; need it now."

As he is talking, a long blast shot out the front window of the cruiser. Next, the left-side windows, shot out.

"We received your message, Sheriff, loud and clear. Sending all available units. Will notify other agencies of your situation. Out."

"Send anyone with a gun!"

"I'll flank him."

"You'll do what, Trigby?"

"Flank him. Go back up the road and come at him from the side."

The Sheriff and Bill Young looked at Trigby for a long moment. "OK, go."

"I'm taking my shotgun. I'll need more shells from the trunk. Fire at that bastard and keep him down."

'Fire at the bastard' is just what Sam and Bill did. Laid down a withering stream of bullets. Trigby leans into the trunk, switches on his flashlight for a second, finds more shells and saw a tube-like contraption that looks odd but lethal. He slams the trunk closed and moves back to the cruiser's side and safety.

Trigby loads his jacket with shotgun shells. "OK, I'm moving out, Sheriff; what the hell is this tube thing?"

"Grenade launcher."

"Grenade laun . . . never mind."

Trigby crawls on his belly until he felt he can't be seen in muzzle flashes from the guns. Then he runs another 40 yards, left the road and heads into the forest. Dark, brushy, unstable footing; everything going against Trigby.

'I am making a hell of a lot of noise.' Actually, Gene Krupa, along with the rest of Benny Goodman's band, could have played at full volume and not been heard over the roar of gunfire.

Trigby, scratched and bleeding from blackberry cuts across his face and hands, makes a slow trek toward the gunfire and finally comes to his target. He can see the muzzle flash from an automatic, ground-mounted machine gun.

'This is not a guy poaching deer.'

Trigby moves deeper into the woods and maneuvers himself behind the machine gun. There are 2 men, the shooter and another, feeding a running belt of shells into the gun.

'Should I shout something? Tell them to stop?' Neither seem a good idea.

Trigby aimed the double-barreled shotgun at the shooter, fires 1 barrel. Moves the gun barrel slightly and fires the other barrel at the 2nd man. Both men down and dead, Trigby made sure.

There is still the sound of gunfire coming from the road. Trigby is worried his friends will shoot him. And it gets worse.

Trigby hears someone coming through the woods, directly at him. No time to reload the shotgun. Drops it and takes his loaded pistol out of a jacket pocket. Whoever is coming at him lets off a shot, way wide. Trigby moves sideways as quick as possible, pistol ready. The next shot from the intruder, followed instantly by Trig's gun, aimed at the muzzle flash. Trigby hears a moan and loud sigh and knows he'd hit the target. Clicks on the flashlight for an instant, looking for signs of breathing. There are none.

"Kommando, Position 2 Berichterstattung, kein Feuer von Position 1. Glauben Sie, dass sie kompromittiert oder tot sind. Vorbei."

"Command, position 2 reporting, no fire coming from position 1. Believe they are compromised or dead. Over."

"Sind die Amerikaner noch da? Vorbei."

"Are the Americans still there? Over."

"Ja, ich feuere immer noch. Vorbei."

"Yes, still firing. Over."

"Feuer nach Belieben. Tötet sie alle."

"Fire at will. Kill them all."

"HEY GUYS, I'M COMING IN; FIRE FROM THIS SIDE ELIMINATED," Trigby shouts.

"PLENTY OF FIRE FROM THE OTHER SIDE OF THE ROAD NOW. COME IN FAST AND DAMMIT, TRIGBY, STOP SHOUTING," is the reply.

Then Trigby had an idea that could change everything. He hustles back to the machine gun. "Damn this is heavy." Trig fell twice getting the gun to the road. Went back for the ammo belts. He finds them under the machine-gunners body and took as much as he could carry. Made it back to the road, barely.

Sweating, nauseous and dead tired, Trigby listened to the fire coming from the other side of the road. He knows the sound; a ground-mounted machine gun. Now his side has 1 too! Next question, how to get it into the fight.

"Guys I got a plan." Trigby said this in a normal tone of voice. No response.

"Guys, I got a plan." A little louder. No response.

"GUYS, I GOT A PLAN. I NEED 1 OF YOU OVER HERE NOW. DON'T ARGUE."

"Sam, why should we rely on the rookie?"

"Well Bill, we don't have a plan and 1 of 2 things are going to happen; either that bastard shooting at us is gonna get lucky, hit the gas tank on this cruiser and we'll be blown to hell. Or we'll run out of ammo and he'll come outa the woods and shoot us between the eyes."

"Well said; let's go with the rookie's plan. Whatever the hell that is."

They argue over who is the fastest runner. 2 guys in their 60's, not much of a choice.

"OK, Bill, cause of your wound, you stay here and give fire. I'll run over to Trigby. You've got 2 double-barreled shotguns here, both loaded. Fire 1 barrel at a time. My long rifles there and a couple of pistols here, all loaded and ready. I showed you how to use the grenade launcher but Bill for god's sake, don't use it unless everything goes to hell."

This conversation is made with machine gun fire hitting the cruiser and the surrounding area.

"Sheriff, I'm sorry it's so dark; I'd sure love to see you run."

"You know, Bill Young, over the last 40 years, I've almost gotten to like you."

"I've got the same feelings for you, Sheriff."

The 2 men shake hands.

'When in the hell is 1 of my ancient comrades going to get here?'

The moment Trigby thought this, a large shape came out of the darkness. Tripped over the machine gun and rolled into the woods.

"Just let me lay here for a bit."

"Sheriff, all I can give you is 30 seconds."

Trigby helps Sam Jacobs up and gets him back on the road.

"I'm handing you ammo belts tha . . . ."

"I know what they are, Trigby. This is all I can carry; I may have to come back for the rest."

"OK, get close behind me but not close enough for both to get hit in 1 blast."

"I'm thinking we should set up here." Trig and the Sheriff are 30 yards to the left of the police cruiser.

"Good spot, Trigby; you're gonna flank the machine gunner over there with this machine gun. Right?"

"Yeah, it's the only thing I remember from the Army and we're going to use the hell out of it."

"Trig, I can see the flash but not good; I need to see more for a better shot." The Sheriff crawled to the right and drug the machine gun with him. He showed Trigby how to stack the ammo belts and feed them into the machine. "I stop firing; you stop feeding, we don't want a jam. And no way this is a poacher's setup. We're into something bigger."

"Where did you get to know machine guns, Sheriff?"

"WW1, basic in Kansas, more training in New York and then France. I'll tell you about it sometime. Are you ready, Trigby?"

"Yes, Sir."

It is as if the Devil came to play with a new toy. The sound of the gun canceling all other sounds, bullets going unceasingly into the side of the weapon and the brilliant flash of the muzzle. In that flash, Trigby can see the Sheriff's face; flash, darkness, flash, darkness. Light and darkness moving very fast. Mesmerizing. In the flashes, the Sheriff looks like the Devil.

This first blast of firing lasts 45 seconds. To Trigby, it seemed an hour, or a lifetime. The Sheriff stopped firing and Trigby stopped feeding. There is no return fire.

Next is a whoosh sound and an explosion (oddly less loud than the machine gun), followed by the unmistakable sound of a tree falling and then screaming.

"Goddammit, Bill, I told you not to use the goddamn launcher. All you did was hit a tree," the Sheriff hissed.

"Seemed to work," Bill's reply.

After a couple more minutes of colorful discourse, Trigby suggests they go to the source of screaming; it had diminished to moaning.

"I'd like to see who we are dealing with."

"Sheriff, stay here, see if your radio still works and get an idea of our ammo and weapons."

"You sure you can make it with your foot, Bill?"

"Hell, I'd walk on my hands to see who these guys are."

Bill and Trigby trudged through the forest, one wounded, both men exhausted.

"I just don't want to get shot, again.

"Not sure if he'll be alive, Bill. Sounds like he's near the end. And if it's like the set-up on the other side of the road, it's at least 2 guys. Got to get there, need to talk to them, find out what the hell is going on."

"Go'in as fast as I can."

Unsure of how many attackers are waiting for them, Bill and Trigby move at a cautious, agonizingly slow pace. They find the 1st dead man, shot at least 4 times from the machine gun's unrelenting fire.

A short distance further is a firing station. Sawn logs, used as a defensive barricade in front of another ground-mounted machine gun. The gun and barricade destroyed by a fallen alder tree.

1 man down behind the machine gun under the tree, moaning softly. Another man 30 feet away, also under the tree. Trigby checks; this man is dead.

The German trooper by the machine gun is alive, not by much, but alive.

"Hilf mir. Hilf mir."

"Help me. Help me."

"Bill, he's speaking German!"

"This son a bitch is German? What the hell is he doing here?"

"I have no idea, Bill but I don't think it's anything good."

Trigby was smart enough to bring the first-aid kit from the Sheriff's cruiser. Shoots the trooper up with morphine and stops some of the bleeding.

"Best I can do. We need to move the tree."

"No way, not until we get some info from him."

Trigby knelt beside the man, removes his helmet, sees the morphine taking effect. Softly he said,

"Can you speak English?"

"What the hell Trigby? Are you German?"

"No Bill, it's all the German I know."

"No . . . Nope."

"And he is telling us he can't speak English."

After several false starts, the German trooper understands the tree won't be lifted until he can explain his actions. This effort is spurred on by Bill Young's cocked pistol in the German's ear.

The language problem is solved with a scrap of paper and a stub of pencil. The German, flat on his back with a large alder tree pinning him to the ground, scrawled a map by flashlight. With additional urging, the trooper details boats, river and large ships. He also gives out the number of troops, by slashes of the pencil.

"This is taking forever. What I get is there are 23 German spies camped by the river waiting for a Liberty ship to go by. Why, I don't know."

"Bill, I'm with you on most of it, but I don't think they are spies; they're too military. I do agree it seems like Liberty ships are a part of this. The most damage would be to try and sink one. I can't see how they could do it from small boats. Hell of a problem if a couple of ships were sunk in the shipping channel. Did you notice the swastika tattoo on his arm? He's going to the next life as a Nazi."

Bill stood up, away from the German trooper. "The best thing we can do now is get this info to the Army, Navy and everybody else."

Trigby shined the flashlight on the trooper and the tree. "First, we need to get the damn tree off this guy."

Bill Young aims his pistol and shoots the German in the head.

"Not now," Bill said.

Trigby couldn't think, hear or see for several minutes. He's always been a healer; today he killed 3 people. And witnessed another killing.

Bill didn't stay around for a discussion. He heads back to the road.

After several more minutes, Trigby followed.

"Position 2, Bericht. Das ist Befehl, Bericht."

"Position 2, report. This is command, report."

No response.

The Sheriff sat off the road, away from the ruined cruiser, gun at the ready. He hears someone coming through the woods.

Bill Young: "Sheriff, I'm coming in."

The Sheriff: "I was gett'in concerned."

When Trigby arrives, he and Bill give the Sheriff a condensed report. There are a few questions.

Sheriff: "How far is this camp?"

Bill Young: "3 miles ahead, maybe."

Sheriff: "And the River?"

Bill Young: "Probably, another 2 miles."

Sheriff: "How is the German that told you all of this?"

Trigby: "Dead."

A conversation at German Command Camp

Commander Hann: "Have we heard from position 1 or 2?"

Sargent: "No. Nothing from either. #1 dropped off first. And then #2. I can send a patrol to determine the condition. But if the US Army is attacking us, we will need every man available, to defend this position."

Commander Hann: "Send the VW, the truck and a squad."

Sargent: "Sir, are you sur__."

Commander Hann: "Send them. Now."

Sargent: "Yes, Sir."

The patrol never returned.

CHAPTER 44

Trigby, Bill Young and the Sheriff lean against what is left of the cruiser.

"Now what?" Sheriff Sam Jacobs with the question all 3 men are thinking.

"Have we heard from our reinforcements?"

"Nope. My radio is busted, and the interior of my beautiful cruiser shot to shit."

"How about ammo and weapons, Sam?"

"4 pistols, 2 long rifles, plenty of ammo for those and the machine gun and ammo belts. Plus the weapons and ammo you're carrying. And, of course, the damn grenade launcher. I found 6 more grenades.

Trigby speaks up, "the Germans must know their 2 machine gun posts are gone. They'll come looking any minute."

"Right – right – let's set up our own machine gun nest – let's get the hell off this road – we need to spread out." The Sheriff and Bill Young with dozens of ideas.

"Boys calm down; I got a plan. Can the cruiser start?"

"No, Trigby it won't. I tried."

"Can we get it into neutral?"

"Let me try. Yep, I got in neutral."

"Perfect, leave it and set the hand brake. Now I need a rag."

"I got a handkerchief." Bill pulled a large Western handkerchief out of his back pocket.

Trigby knells down and reaches under the ruined cruiser. He sees a leak in the gas tank and soaks the rag in gasoline.

"Bill, you and I will push this wreck about 40 yards further. After that, the road drops fast to the river."

"Are you planning on rolling the cruiser down the hill into the Germans?"

"I'm figuring they'll be coming up here in some sort of vehicle."

"Maybe you should have Sam help you; I'm pretty much done in."

"Sorry Bill, Sam will be setting up the machine gun on that small rise," Trigby pointed forward to the left side of the road.

"Sam, got it?"

"Yep, Trig I'm on it."

"Shit they are coming." The noise of an approaching, slow-moving vehicle can be heard.

"Bill, you gotta do this. Take the strap off your rifle and tie it to the steering wheel and the door handle. I want this cruiser pointed straight ahead, all the way down the hill."

"Think this'll work, Trigby?"

"I'm praying it will."

To Bill and Trigby, pushing the cruiser 40 yards seemed like 40 miles. The cruiser, perched on the top of the hill ready to go once the hand brake is lifted. Bill's handkerchief hanging out the gas pipe, Zippo lighter ready.

Up ahead, Sam set up the machine gun. He has a good line of fire; his killing zone started halfway up the hill. The only problem he can't control is loading the gun, then firing and reloading by himself. With no one feeding the ammo belts, there will be short bursts, no prolonged fire.

Trigby sees the half-lights on the road. 2 vehicles, a truck and a jeep.

"Bill get ready."

Bill had been leaning over, hands on his knees, breathing hard, vomiting twice.

"I'm ready now, dammit. Then I'm gonna die."

Waiting till the German vehicles started up the hill, Trigby and Bill push hard at the back of the cruiser. As it begins to roll, Trigby lights the handkerchief. Amazingly the cruiser stays on the road. Halfway down the hill, the gas tank blew. It hit the truck as a flaming mass of gasoline and steel. Germans leapt out of the truck, some on fire.

"What do we do now, Trigby?"

"Run like hell."

Bill can't run; he can only limp. Trig helps him to the side of the road, across from Sam.

"Bill, you are on your own here. I'm going to help Sam with the machine gun. Good luck to you."

"Back at you, Trigby. Give'em hell." Bill has a shotgun, long rifle, pistol and his new favorite weapon, the grenade launcher, with ammunition for each.

Trigby got to Sam just in time to feed the ammo belt into the gun. "You're loaded, Sheriff." Sam Jacobs opens up with the machine gun when the Jeep gets halfway up the hill.

The Germans in the Jeep moves past the burning truck and comes up the hill at high speed. The first blast from Sam's machine gun takes out the headlights and apparently some part of the engine. The Jeep comes to a stop with smoke pouring out of the hood.

Sam Jacobs works on the men running from the Jeep. He hits most of them and then goes back to the Jeep.

Sam and Trigby hear the woosh of a grenade leaving the launcher and, in an instant, the Jeep explodes.

"Trigby, that damn Bill will set the forest on fire with those grenades."

"Not sure; his aim is getting better."

"What now?"

"Not sure, Sheriff. Keep on the lookout for these assholes coming up through the woods. I'm going to check on Bill."

Trigby sprinted, well not really a sprint, across the road and dove behind Bill.

"How come there's no fire coming from over there, Trig?"

"Nothing to shoot at. You blew everyone up."

"Bullshit, I'm watching 1 of those bastards now." Bill had the long rifle's scope up to his eye. "He's trying to get away. Try'n to get across the road."

A dark figure ran in front of the burning Jeep. The flames behind him outlined the man. Bill pulls the trigger. The figure drops.

"Got him."

"How are you feeling, Bill?"

"Awful, which is an improvement."

"We need to figure out what to do next. Any ideas?"

"Trigby, you are the planner in this operation. I'm just a foot soldier; a foot soldier shot in the foot."

"Well, I'm torn; retreat might be the best idea. Or__"

"I hate best ideas."

"Or we can press on. Still, lots of ammo; you could blast something else with your grenades."

"Happy to do that."

The Naselle Fire Department decided for Trigby.

Bill and Trigby hear the sirens first, then saw the flashing lights.

"What the hell is that?"

"Our rescue attack team."

"Guess it's not a surprise attack."

The fire engine roars past Trigby, Bill and Sam's position. Armed men are clinging to the fire engine for dear life.

Next, trucks and cars with every able-bodied male in both Wahkiakum and Pacific counties. The reason they are so late in their rescue is after the fire was out, everybody had to go home for weapons. Shotguns, pistols, revolvers and deer rifles. Weapons used every hunting season. Weapons not used for years. Every car and truck window rolled down, muzzles sticking out.

Risking his life, Trigby jumped in front of the Naselle Fire Chief's truck. Luckily the Chief, Lenard Larsen, knew Trigby.

"Trigby, what in the hell are you doing out here?"

"I'll tell you in a minute, Len. First, you got to stop these guys from going any further. Do you have communication with your fire engine?"

"Of course, I do."

"Tell them to stop."

"Why should___."

"They will die. Shot to death from heavy fire."

That got the Chief, Lenard Larsen's attention. Trigby told him the whole story in a 2-minute verbal blast. The Chief got the fire engine on his radio and told them to stop and turn around.

"Can't do it, Chief, roads not wide enough. Over."

"Get those men off the truck and spread out on both sides of the road. Expect heavy incoming fire soon."

And that got the attention of every man on the fire engine.

Sam Jacobs makes a radio call from the Fire Chief's truck to Fort Canby. It did not go well.

"This is the second call for men and weapons. Are they on the way?"

"Yes, Sheriff, we sent a Jeep and 3 MPs, but they had a flat tire on the way. I can contact them and find out their position."

"Son, I know you don't report to me, but if I don't get soldiers and weapons here damn fast, the position of my boot will be up your ass. I got a bunch of old men here with antique weapons they haven't used since they were kids. Against an enemy force of unknown number. I can't stay on this damn radio forever; you tell your command we are in a shooting war for the 2nd time, and this time we will return fire to the enemy whether your command helps us or not."

"Well said, Sam."

"Thank you, Trigby. Can't imagine the US Army too happy about having a small-town hick Sheriff tell'em how to run a war. But I'm starting to get pissed off."

The Fire Chief and Sheriff have a pow-wow about the next step.

"Sam, I got a lot of men and weapons. Not sure of the ammo and, to be honest, not so sure of the men. How about you?"

"Chief, here is what my guys have; a couple or 3 shotguns, couple or 3 long rifles and pistols. Also, a German ground-mounted machine gun and an American grenade launcher. Ammo for everything."

"Holy shit, Sam, you're fighting a war up here!"

"Exactly, and it is not over. The Germans aren't here to invade Skamokawa; they have something much bigger in mind. I think it has to do with Liberty ships on the River. I'm also thinking it will happen tonight. Maybe right now."

"Old men and antique guns?"

"Yep, but we can't wait for 3 MP's. We go with what we have. Now."

"I agree. What do you have in mind?"

"Our biggest assets are the fire engine and machine gun."

"Agreed."

"Does your pumper still have water on board?"

"Half full at most."

"Could a stream of water knock a man down?"

"Sure and probably disable his weapon. Hell, if he opens his mouth, might drown."

"Where on the fire engine can we mount the machine gun?"

"Well, I suppose we could lower the windshield, mount the legs on the engine hood. What side does it feed from?"

"Left."

"OK, this could work. The driver feeds the ammo into the gun and the shooter sits on the right-hand seat. Course, it won't work if the truck is moving."

"Got it, Chief. Let's get weapons, ammo, myself, Trigby and Bill Young into your truck and get down there."

"That's a hell'uva group, Sam."

The Sheriff isn't sure if this is a positive or negative remark.

The fighting crew is positioned around the fire engine, ready for action. Or near as ready as they will ever be. Driving past the burned-out truck, the Jeep and cruiser gave everyone a realistic view of what could be coming.

2 firemen stand on each side of the fire engine, fire hoses in their hands. The fire engine isn't moving but running to keep the water pressure up. The driver got off and Trigby took his place. Sam Jacobs climbs up into the right-side seat. Bill Young took a fire axe and instead of lowering it, smashed out the windshield.

"*Ah, Jesus,*" the Fire Chief mumbled to himself.

"Trig, this might work. But once it starts firing, not sure I can keep it from sliding off the hood."

"Bill, you see any duct tape around?"

"How in the hell would I know? CHIEF, GOT ANY DUCT TAPE ON THIS RIG?"

"Locker on your left."

The machine gun is duct taped down.

Bill's shouting brought no rebuke. There is so much talking, so much moving around in the bushes that the Germans could be near, in plain sight and nobody would hear or see them.

And there are Germans very near and in plain sight. 3 of them, armed at the side of the road next to the fire engine.

"Hey, you!" The fireman, holding a high-velocity fire hose, shouts and the 3 men raise their weapons. Water at an extremely high pressure shoots out from the hose. Knocked 2 of the intruders flat. The 3rd made a hasty exit back into the woods. Shot in the back by a fusillade from half of the assembled men. And then everyone starts firing, shooting into the woods.

"DAMMIT TO HELL. STOP SHOOTING. SAVE YOUR AMMO; YOU WILL NEED IT."

The Sheriff and Fire Chief have to make the same demand several times before the shooting stopped. All 3 Germans, dead. Amazingly no Americans hit by friendly fire.

"Commander Hann, the truck and Jeep are destroyed; all men on both vehicles, dead, wounded or missing."

"Damn it. Giese, form a protection ring around the command center. 200 yards out. Depending on their strength, we will stand our ground until the Liberty ship is near. Then we retreated to the River. Do you understand these orders?"

"Yes, Commander."

Obersturmbannfuhrer Hann is still very much in charge. He knows he can fulfill his mission. Like every other mission, this one has its obstacles. Hann isn't angry or disappointed at what is happening. He is moving, positively, toward his goal.

"They must be stopped. Jukka, get a damn rifle and act like a damn soldier. Giese, take him with you."

"What's next?"

Another pow-wow; this time, Trigby and Bill Young are included. Trigby has the scrap of paper with the map of the German's positions. The map is passed around and discussed; quickly.

"Here's what we need to do." Bill waits until he has everyone's attention.

"What do you have, Bill?"

"A plan out of Trigby's playbook, we flank'em. Trigby and I and anybody dumb enough to join us, move through the woods down to the River. End up on the West side of their boats. We attack from there."

"I'm liking this," said Trigby.

"Then," Bill had more. "Everybody else hits the German's command camp. Not sure how many enemy troops are there, but hell can't be more than the parade we have."

"And the machine gun will be a big plus," says the Sheriff.

"Unless they have more machine guns," this from the Fire Chief.

"Regardless, we move now," from Trigby.

"Bill, I'm begging you not to go; you need to get off that foot."

"Nope, I wrapped it in duct tape, Trig, can't feel it now."

"That's exactly what I'm worried about."

"I'm going now . . . . you going?"

Of course, Trigby goes with Bill and they take 3 hand-picked long-time hunters, all great marksmen. The hike through the woods is daunting, particularly for Bill. Trigby and the others leave Bill to hike on his own.

At last, the 4 men, minus Bill, reach the River. Bust through the brush, down a steep sand dune and onto the beach. Tide running low, the beach, spotted with small ponds, some leaking rivulets, running down to the River. No sign of Nazis.

"Let's head upriver, keep close to the dunes; I don't want us spotted against the water," Trigby in charge. He doesn't think about being in charge; it just came naturally.

As Trigby and his crew scrambled through the dark forest, the Sheriff, Fire Chief and armed locals moved slowly down the road. Headlights off, the fire engine creeps forward. In front of the fire engine, on each side of the road, are 2 men, rifles loaded, safeties off, searching the woods. The rest of the locals are behind the fire engine. This procession moves ahead.

According to the map, the Nazi command camp is just off the road to the left. Sheriff Sam Jacobs sends 5 men into the woods to get on the East side of the camp. The rest of the men and fire engine head directly for the camp. They don't get far.

Small arms fire comes from both sides of the road. The Sheriff opens up with the machine gun, spraying fire to 1 side of the road and then the other.

The Nazis hold off firing until the Americans are close. These troopers are a tested fighting team. Jukka can't believe they allowed the enemy this close.

"Fire!" The 1st volley surprises Jukka. The return fire from the Americans more so. Then his training comes to him. Kill or be killed.

Trigby and the others heard the gunfire.

"We need to move fast now, the Germans will try to punch through our guys, or they'll try to get away on the River. Either way, we need to get close and stop them."

There are lights ahead, near the River.

"Go ahead, guys; I can't keep up. Fire at the lights; if there are boats, fire at them."

Now on his own, Trigby trudges forward. It isn't about moving fast; it's about continuing to move.

The 3 hunters get close enough to see that the lights are flashlights. The men spread apart. Kneel, take careful aim.

"Let it go!"

3 shots ring out, then 3 more shots. No return fire. 2 Germans fall to the ground. Another round from the Americans. Scattered return fire.

"Look at the River, is that a boat? Look through your scope." Trigby has caught up.

"Yeah, small boat, like a rowboat but thinner. Couple of guys, 1 rowing, the other guy trying to start the motor."

"In your range?"

"Yup, but how do we know they're Ger___."

"Fire now, aim low, sink the boat. All of you, fire now."

The boat sank, 2 Germans shot; 1 standing in the boat, the other shot in the water.

"OK, spread out, move forward. Be careful."

The Sheriff and the Fire Chief are in a firefight of their own. Heavy fire coming from the Nazi command camp. Sam, the Sheriff, on the fire engine blasting away with the machine gun. Sweep after sweep, side to side. The driver of the fire engine who had taken over for Trigby fed the voracious machine gun yard after yard of shells. Tired, worn out, standing in the open cockpit, the 2 men had forgotten fear and fatigue, replaced with 1 mission, feed the beast and keep it firing.

The Fire Chief has locals lying on the ground on both sides of the fire engine. The 1st volley from the American locals is formidable but generally off-target with many inoperable weapons and old ammunition.

The Americans have a greater number but the Nazis are a thoroughly professional fighting force. Itching to fight. And fight they do. Measured and violent.

"Take good aim, look for muzzle flashes, don't shoot wildly, conserve ammo; we may have to shoot our way out of here." The Chief's directions are sometimes heard, sometimes not; sometimes followed, sometimes not. The locals did have a common goal, to get out of this alive.

"Chief, how we doing?"

"Good God, Bill. You scared the daylight out of me! Get down."

"If I got down, don't think I'd get back up. Where's that fire coming from?"

"The bastards have a camp about 200 yards to the Southeast."

"Any of our guys between us and the camp, Chief?"

"Nope, 5 men of ours, to the east of the camp."

"Got it." And with that, Bill is gone.

'Where in the hell is that guy going?' the Chief thought.

Bill climbs up into the cockpit. Scared the driver/machine gun feeder, but he managed to keep loading.

"Sheriff, where is this camp?"

"What___?". Sam stopped firing. "Dammit, I thought you went with Trigby."

"Got tired of falling on my ass in the woods. Point to where it is."

"Right there."

"About 200 yards?"

"Could be. Sure."

This back and forth goes on with incoming fire all around the 3 men in the fire engine. Standing in full view, no cover. It makes one wonder if God takes sides.

Bill loads a grenade into the launcher, lifts the barrel skyward. Looks like a golfer on the 1st tee. The sound of the grenade leaving the barrel can't be heard; the explosion can. The reload is fast, followed by the 2nd explosion.

Incoming fire slows and then sputters out.

"Holy shit, Bill, you're like a gunslinger with that thing."

"Thanks, Sheriff. Couple of grenades left."

"OK, everybody, let's advance, carefully. There could be a lot of these bastards left."

The fire engine and local brigade followed the Sheriff's advice, inching forward.

But the Sheriff is wrong; the few remaining Nazi troops are retreating to the River.

Trigby and his group on the beach are moving slowly. Closer and closer to the small cluster of boats defended by Nazi troopers. All at once, fire coming from the Nazis increases dramatically. Pinning down Trigby and a guy from Naselle.

"Hey, what the hell happened? It's like they had a squadron that just woke up."

Trigby had a damn good idea where these new enemy fighters came from.

"I think the Sheriff and Fire Chief have overrun their camp."

Trigby is right. The Nazis are in full withdrawal, heading for the River. The Americans, right behind, closing fast. The fire engine, loaded with armed locals, stops at the top of a steep dune, looking down at the beach.

"I'm aiming the machine gun at troops and the boats. They must have a plan for boats." Sam said this as Bill Young loads his launcher. Bill says, "tell me when I can send a grenade in."

The machine gun quiets the fire coming from the Nazis. They are now facing Americans on 3 sides; Trigby and his group on the West, the 5 men Sam sent to the East side are now in place on the beach, the fire engine and locals are in an ideal firing position on the North and the River guards their escape to the South.

"It's like shooting fish in a barrel; not sure it's right," said 1 of the locals.

"Well, hell, walk on down and ask if they want to surrender," said his buddy.

Bill, a little bit miffed about the delay in firing his last 2 grenades, finally gets the OK. 2 nicely placed blasts destroy boats and Nazis.

The silence is eerie. No gunfire, still too dark to see clearly. The 3 groups of Americans close in carefully. Worried about getting shot by the last remaining Nazi. And worried more about being shot by friendly fire.

A splash, sounding like a boat being launched. Oars in the water.

"Where is that?"

"Over there."

"Over there, where?"

1 of Trig's sharpshooters spots a boat heading for the middle of the River. Uses his scope, takes careful aim, pulls the trigger. 1 German down; the German is Oberstrum Giese. He is dead.

Now everybody spots the boat and opens fire. The boat sinking, another Nazi jumps overboard.

"STOP FIRING, DAMMIT WE NEED HIM ALIVE!"

With blood lust running high, it takes a bit of time for the firing to stop. Bill wishes he had 1 more grenade.

The Nazi knows there is no escape; he swims toward the beach. Comes out of the water, striding forcefully to the large group of American irregulars.

"I am Oberstrumbannfuher Hann of the German SS Expeditionary Force. I surrender under the Geneva Rules of War.

The Sheriff led the German off the beach and tied him to the Fire engine.

His whereabouts after that are unknown.

EPILOGUE

The men who fought the *'Battle of the Columbia'* have not been recognized for their valor. In fact, officially, the whole episode never happened. A week after the battle, when stories grew to epic proportions, 4 gentlemen (they did not look all that gentle) from the Federal Bureau of Investigation visited Naselle and the surrounding area. Stayed for a month and talked with every man who claimed to be a part of the battle.

In no uncertain terms, the FBI agents made the point that any discussion, written or oral, regarding the episode was unlawful. Something about the US Secret War Time Act; a federal crime, with federal jail time and a federal-size fine.

There were several dissenters, but the rejoinder *'we will be taking you to the FBI office in Portland in handcuffs now'* brought all discussion to an end.

There wasn't any official death toll, nor is there one now. The closest anyone has come, is 18 Americans dead. 3 by friendly fire, 12 by German fire and 3 by heart attack. The number of Americans wounded, bruised, limbs sprained or broken and/or scared shit-less is unknown, but is believed to be a big, big, number.

On the German side, of the 24 fighters, including Jukka; only 2 are believed to have survived; Commander Hann and Jukka.

Just before the Americans descended on the German Command Center, Jukka, assigned to a small squad led by Scharfuher Giese, merely walked away from the fighting. He walked North-East, between the Americans on the gravel road and the Americans on the beach to the East. Jukka walked away from everything. His Army, Homeland and Furher. And his hopes for a better, different life. And he left behind his beloved Dea.

Jukka traveled across the States, hitch-hiked, jumped freight trains, and stayed in towns long enough to get a job and save some money. Oddly, when the town and job seemed to be working out, he took off again. Traveled through the mid-West, then down the East coast. Stayed in New Orleans the longest, earning enough to buy a car.

Eventually, Jukka's travels brought him back to Astoria, as he knew they would. He parked his Ford coupe at the Portway Tavern and went in for a beer. Trying to get his courage up, he had another. Thought about a 3rd but knew he had to go now or never.

Jukka walked to the Dough Boy monument and turned right and then left. Looked up the steep stairs at Veiko's house. A different color now. Jukka's whole life had brought him here. As he stood, looking up from the street, the front door opened and an adult Dea, holding a baby in her arms, came out. Followed by a tall man, blond and strong, with a fair-haired boy at his side.

Jukka turned quickly and walked away.

"Trigby Newton, why do I have to always point out the obvious to you."

"Someone has to, obviously."

"If you are going to be a smart aleck, I can stop right now. And you can continue living in the basement of a Church, like you are just passing through. Not willing to stand up like a grown man and get on with the rest of your life. With a beautiful woman, you don't deserve, waiting a ridiculous amount of time for 1 question from you."

"Somehow, you don't seem to have the empathetic, quiet-toned message that I enjoy so much from your husband, the Pastor."

"That's why he's the Pastor and I'm not. And right now, you need my message."

"And that message is?"

"Marry the woman or I will beat your head in with the frying pan you gave me for Christmas. There, is that empathetic enough for you?"

"I've been think___"

"Stop thinking and do it. Now!

The wedding was held in the backyard of Sally's home. A small, quiet affair. With Jenny as Sally's maid of honor. Sandy and Teddy stood up for Trigby as his 'best dogs.' Both Trigby and dogs wore bow ties. Pastor Lawson officiated.

Helen made a wonderful wedding cake, and if not for the beautiful bride, it would have stolen the show. Sam and Lenard, Sheriff and Fire Chief, could not agree on whose entrée was best. Sam, salmon with secret sauce on top. Lenard, smoked salmon. And yes, the salmon were in season, swimming in the Columbia River the day before.

The years passed. Trigby retired first, then Sally. She really didn't want to; knew she would miss the kids. But she didn't want to leave Trigby at home alone. Worried he would remodel the entire house, starting with the roof and working his way down.

The 2 of them at home, together. Those were pleasant years. They traveled some but always found that where they lived was better than where they visited.

Trigby went first. Late in the fall, on a night that reminded everyone that winter was coming, he told Sally;

"I'm heading up to bed; you tuckered me out with all the chores."

"Trigby, are you talking about napping on the couch most of the morning and then taking out the garbage?"

"Yes, like I said, tuckered me out."

When Sally came to bed an hour later, Trigby was gone. Died in his sleep.

And now Sally, alone, again. She did have her friends, many friends. Teacher and student friends. Church friends at Peace Lutheran, the Lawsons' church. When the Lawson's daughter, Jenny, married, Sally was her Maid of Honor. With the birth of Jenny's son, Sally and Helen Lawson battled, politely, over who got the most time watching the child. In the end, they both spoiled the baby together.

"You will spoil my boy rotten, if you 2 don't knock it off," Jenny's refrain. Sally and Helen's reply, said in unison sometimes, "we are OK with that."

Sally felt her death coming on. Not like a bad cold coming, but a feeling she was moving on, to something different. She didn't think of it as something better, for she had lived a wonderful life. And was thankful for it. From that 1st feeling, she died 2 months later.

Jenny, her husband and son live on Sally's farm, given to Jenny in Sally's will. Jenny's son will grow up as a farm boy, not a city kid. The other important part of the family is the German Shepard, called Teddy, sometimes Teddy #4 and sometimes just 4.

Trigby and Sally are buried in the Elsie Cemetery, next to Trigby's first family. Sally thought it fair for all the years she had with Trigby that they missed.

Jim Hallaux was born & raised in Astoria, Oregon. He lives there now with his wife, Robbie & dog Oak. Jim enjoys writing, reading, cooking & 'Dog Golf...'

Oak and the author. (She won!)

Made in the USA
Columbia, SC
20 May 2023

16376427R00202